I0760933

TIME FOR CHANGE

WESTERN TIME TRAVEL ROMANCE

NIKI J. MITCHELL

TIME FOR CHANGE

A gorgeous, good-hearted cowboy from 1887 falls for a modern, adventurous elementary teacher.

Zack Fairfield hates living a lie, but that's what this time traveling cowboy must do to fit into the 21st century. He catches his secret crush's attention—until she heads for Colorado at the end of the summer.

Birdie Kellogg isn't looking for a relationship—just a summer fling with her brother's best friend.

She isn't looking to move back home.

She isn't looking to get pregnant.

But it happens anyway.

Then she attempts to meet with the father of the child only to discover he had returned to the past.

What else could go wrong?

***Time for Change* is a complete stand-alone and can be read without reading any of the other books or spin-off series, but if you prefer to read in order, start with *Time to Save the Cowboy* as the characters and families do inter-connect.**

This book is dedicated to my friends, family, and readers. Thank you for your support.

Niki

CHAPTER 1

Hot damn, the best man is a hunk.

Roberta Kellogg shouldn't be distracted by the handsome guy at her brother's wedding, but really, how could she resist studying that tall drink of water in a tux? The suit molded to Zack's broad shoulders and brawny build. The fact that Birdie had to angle her neck back to see his face meant he stood at least a head taller than her.

Oh, what a face.

His bronzed complexion was a stark contrast to the crisp white shirt with its stiff collar. His square jaw featured a hint of a five o'clock shadow. And his wondrous lips were full for a man but sexy, nonetheless. His light brown slicked back hair added to his GQ hotness, and she could imagine him on their front cover. As if sensing her, his eyes connected with hers and twinkled with mischief as his mouth quirked upward.

She flashed him a smile and imagined his large hands roving along her body. A breeze from the Majestic River blew against her cheek.

"With this ring," she heard Garrett utter.

Focus on the wedding.

That lasted maybe ten seconds.

She glanced sideways at the audience. Over a hundred chairs lined both sides of an aisle covered with a white runner. In the front row her dad held her niece on his lap and whispered something into Charlotte's ear.

Next to him, her mother beamed at the couple as they said their vows. Garrett had always been her favorite and from Birdie's perspective could do no wrong. Unlike her.

The ludicrous pink and ivory rosette corsage tickled her wrist, and she fiddled with the lace. The pink matched her frilly bridesmaid gown that made her look like a flamingo. Well, at least she had company in her awful attire. Her cousin, best friend, and sister-in-law all had matching dresses.

"You may kiss the bride." Underneath a make-shift arch adorned with ivory and blush-colored roses, her brother secured his arms around Josie's waist and dipped her back; her veil flowing in the breeze as they kissed.

"It is with great honor that I present to you—Mr. and Mrs. Garrett Kellogg."

The guests applauded.

The bride and groom glided down the aisle. Her younger brother, Henry, offered his arm. It still surprised Birdie that she'd been included in the wedding party. Except for the occasional FaceTime and phone calls, she hardly knew her brother's bride. But Josie said she belonged.

Her heart warmed at the gesture.

"Bridal party, over here for photos." The photographer motioned toward a canopy of trees. The guests headed east to the large open aired tent which served as the reception area.

"Move in a little closer. That's it." The photographer posed the bride and groom on a grassy knoll overlooking the river.

Surveying her view of the whole valley from this spot on the Silver Spur Ranch, she imagined galloping along the trails through the hills and enjoying the sun shining down on her. Maybe she'd see a deer attending to her fawns or a lop-eared jack hopping along the path. Nature at its finest.

"Come on, sis." Henry brought her toward their group of friends and family congregating under an oak tree.

One of Birdie's pointy heels dug into the ground. She wobbled but caught herself. How women went all day in these shoes was beyond her. If only she could have worn her sneakers or better yet, hiking boots.

Dad had his back to her isolating himself near the edge of a hill. She couldn't help smiling. Laura and Jacob Kellogg were quite different in personality. Her mom loved to be the center of attention, while her dad never cared for crowds.

Dropping her hold on her brother's arm, she headed over to him. "Hi."

Her dad enveloped her in his arms, and she leaned against his strong shoulders, the same shoulders she had leaned on so many times in the past. "It's nice to have you home. Even if it's only a couple of days."

"Thank you." A twinge of guilt knotted her stomach. *I'll never measure up, Dad.* She really should come home more often she decided as she stepped out of his hold.

Mother walked over to them. Her lips pressed together for a nanosecond but quickly flashed into a practiced smile as she kissed her dad's cheek. "It was a lovely ceremony."

"Yes, it was." With her mom, the less she said the better.

"We need the parents over here," the photographer announced.

The bride and groom were kissing—again. Yep, those two were definitely in love. She let out a sigh as she joined the others gathered underneath a tree, squeezing into a spot between her best friend Kristy and cousin Mia. "Hey."

"Great wedding." Kristy bounced on her toes.

"Almost as wonderful as ours." Mia kissed Dusty's cheek.

"I totally agree." Dusty put his arm around Mia and brought her closer.

Marriage seemed to agree with her cousin and brother. Birdie couldn't see herself tied down. Colorado suited her. Teaching ten months a year in a party town fit her lifestyle. Line dancing or club hopping with friends. Hiking in the fall.

Snowboarding in the winter. River rafting in the spring. Trail riding in the summer. Her life was full.

"Clint's here." Kristy's lips quirked up into a smirk. "Can't wait to party with him."

"You mean the wavy-haired guy in the third row you kept checking out during the ceremony?" Birdie asked.

"Was I that obvious?"

"Yes. But I doubt he minded."

"Hey, Birdie. Good seeing you again." Zack inched into the empty space to her right.

"You, too." She caught a whiff of his spicy cologne. Her cheeks heated like a mini inferno. Her equilibrium shifted like the bottom falling out of a Gravitron carnival ride, making it hard to stand because the guy's smoking. She had noticed him the last Christmas she came home but had been too busy dodging her mother to take a closer look. But now. Wow. Talk about sexy,

Stay calm. Play it cool.

"Wish you didn't have to leave tomorrow night," Kristy said.

"I thought about staying another day. Unfortunately, all the direct flights were booked for Monday."

"You spending any time here this summer?" Zack lifted a brow.

"I don't think so. Actually, one of my friends just bought a speed boat. A group of us have planned several trips water skiing at the lake. You guys should come for a visit." Birdie motioned to Kristy and Zack.

"I'm in." He winked.

The idea of seeing his wet, sinewy body in a pair of swimming trunks behind a ski boat made her hot. She fanned her face.

"Bridesmaids. You're next," the photographer called.

"Come on, girl. Let's dazzle the camera with our beauty." Kristy took her arm.

Birdie added an extra sway in her walk. The photos went fast. Josie posed with her brother Dusty. Then the photographer called the Kellogg family.

"Stand straighter. You're slouching a little, sweetie," her mother whispered in her ear and moved on the other side of the groom next to her father.

Her stomach tightened listening to the reprimand. She immediately set her shoulders back. Ten years of beauty pageant training were ingrained in her brain.

"Don't let her get to you," Henry said quietly. Bless her youngest brother.

"I'm not." To keep her aggravation from showing, she fiddled with her wrist corsage.

Several minutes later, the whole wedding party posed together. The bride and bridesmaids were in the front row, the groom and groomsmen in the back.

Zack stood directly behind her, and she couldn't help looking over her shoulder.

"Promise me a dance." His warm breath tickled her neck.

"You've got it." Maybe more than one.

"Alright everyone, say *cowboy wedding*," the photographer said.

After countless clicks, the picture taking was finally over.

"Let's get this party started." Birdie linked her arm through Kristy's, and they headed underneath the fluttering canopy. Strings of lights twinkled off crystal champagne glasses. Flames from candles shone inside pink-colored tumblers.

"The bar's in the back corner." Kristy didn't waste any time weaving them through clusters of people toward their destination.

CHAPTER 2

Zack sat next to the groom at a long table at the side of the room under a humongous canvas canopy. A melodic laugh filled the air, one that belonged to his best friend's sister, Birdie, a.k.a. the goddess. At least that's what he considered her to be ever since he first saw her two years ago at Christmas. He'd been crushing on her all this time, but she never seemed to notice him—until this weekend. Unable to stop leaning forward, his focus drifted past his cousin to Birdie.

Viewing her from afar, she gave him a sly smile. The kind of smile that brightens up the room. And this smile seemed to be just for him.

He got lost in her plum-colored lips. Would they be as velvety soft as they looked against his mouth? He hoped to find out tonight.

His cock twitched.

Garrett nudged him, taking him out of his daydream. "Can't believe I'm married."

"You found a good one." Zack was happy for his friend.

"I have a feeling you'll be next."

"Not me. I like being a bachelor." A less complicated life worked for him.

"That's what I used to say."

"Shouldn't you be concentrating on that new bride of yours?" This conversation was getting weird especially after he had been ogling Garrett's sister. Thankfully his friend hadn't noticed.

"We're just fine." Garrett set his arm around Josie's shoulders.

Zack took a bite of chicken covered in a white sauce. "This is good."

"I'd rather have steak," Henry, Garrett's younger brother called out.

"When you get married you can select whatever menu you damn well please." Garrett laughed.

"Such language," Josie swatted his arm playfully. Knowing his friend, she'd heard a hell of a lot worse.

"Sorry, Mrs. Kellogg. I sure like the sound of that." Garrett pressed his mouth against his wife's lips.

"Save some for the honeymoon." Henry scrunched up his face. "About that, where are you guy's going again?"

"San Diego," Garrett said.

"Why not Hawaii? I've heard the waves are awesome," Henry asked.

Josie blinked twice. Zack got her angst. As a fellow time traveler, she probably preferred to keep her feet on the ground.

"Why waste hours on a plane when we're booked right on the beach at the Coronado Hotel?" Garrett squeezed Josie's hand.

"Love that place. You know, it's supposedly haunted." Mia put both hands in the air and wiggled her fingers in an eerie motion.

"No ghost is gonna bother us. My wife won't tolerate anyone ruining our honeymoon."

Since Josie used to live in the bunkhouse, Zack had seen her tenacity firsthand.

The meal went on. Eventually, the servers collected the dinner plates.

Garrett nudged Zack. "Ready for your speech?"

"Yep." Zack pulled out a paper from his vest pocket.

Far too many guests were seated at circular tables. He fought off the worry in his gut. Public speaking wasn't on his list of favorites. Still, part of his job as best man was to give this speech, and he wasn't about to shirk his responsibilities. Using his spoon, he made a tink-tink-tink against his champagne glass. It took maybe ten seconds to get everyone's attention. Their eyes all fixed on him.

He swallowed hard, sucked in a deep breath, and said, "I'm Zack Fairfield." He glanced down at his paper. "I can honestly say Garrett is handsome, brilliant, funny, and char …" He turned toward his friend. "Garrett, what's the last word? I can't read your writing."

Garrett rolled his eyes while the guests laughed.

He turned his head and studied Birdie. Their eyes collided, hypnotizing him in the depth of the emerald color. He quickly looked away and concentrated on the page in his hand. "Anyway, Garrett's been a good friend for the last few years, and I'm happy he found Josie. For those of you who don't know how they met, Garrett was acting as town sheriff for the Founder's Day Celebration when he arrested her and threw her in a jail cell."

Someone gasped.

"To be fair, he thought she was the mayor's daughter." It had been a crazy day. "Garrett more than made amends for his mistake—including slipping a ring on her finger several months later. These two belong together. To the bride and groom."

In unison everyone repeated the words and glasses clinked. He wiped a hand across his forehead. Whew. That was intense.

Kristy spoke next. "I've only known Josie for a little over a year, but it seems like we've been friends forever. She's not only sweet but makes line dancing a blast, especially when she ends up turning the wrong way."

"I'm getting better." Josie blushed.

"That you are. It didn't take long for her to fall for Garrett."

Zack couldn't help flicking his gaze to Birdie.

She smiled.

"Now for my words of wisdom. May you guys share everything together … including laundry … dishes … feeding livestock … and shoveling manure." Only Kristy would come up with a weird line like that. "To the bride and groom." She held up her glass and the guests joined in.

Garrett's dad toasted the couple. The man's proud stance reminded Zack of his pa at his oldest brother's wedding. An ache stabbed through his heart. He missed his family.

The band announced the first dance. "Forever and Always" played for the newlyweds. He watched the groom spin his new bride, an enormous grin across his face.

The next song had Garrett dancing with his mother, while his father danced with Josie. In a few minutes, the whole Kellogg clan joined in.

"Come on, cuz." Kristy snagged his arm and brought him onto the floor. "What's up with you and Birdie? You guys have been eyeing each other all day."

"Nothing."

"If you say so." Kristy tilted her head. "Too bad she lives in Colorado."

"It sounds like a great place to visit." They glided across the floor.

"You'd really go there?"

He shrugged.

"You've gotta do it. Take some time off for a change."

"Has anyone ever told you you're as tenacious as a bulldog?" He spun her under his arm.

"Nope, but thanks for the compliment."

The song changed to a fast two-step. Zack moved in front of Birdie. "Wanna dance?"

"Sure."

He offered his hand. Their fingertips touched and a sizzle zinged right through him. She relaxed into him as he took the lead and got a whiff of her tantalizing honeysuckle perfume.

"You're a good dancer," Birdie said.

"Thanks." He twirled her under his arm and pulled her tight against him. "Kristy says you're leaving tomorrow night."

"I am."

"I've never been to Colorado. Besides water skiing, what else is there to do?"

"Snowboarding and cross country in the winter. Tons of water sports during spring and summer. Plenty of ranches to visit when I get an urge to go riding."

"Sounds like paradise." He snagged her a little closer. She fit perfectly in his arms.

"For me it is. Can I ask you something? It's kinda personal."

"Ask away."

"I know you're Kristy's cousin. We've been friends since grade school, but she didn't mention you until a few years ago."

Not about to say he'd been living in 1887, he gave a fairly close version of the truth. "I was bored with living in Cedar Springs and decided to visit my aunt and uncle."

"And you liked Surprise Valley so much you decided to stay?" Her voice came out breathy.

"Something like that."

The song ended and her dad walked up. "May I have this dance?"

Her eyes sparkled. "Of course, Dad."

"In that case, let's show 'em how it's done."

Zack stepped away and headed for the bar more than ready for a cold beer.

CHAPTER 3

"It seems like only yesterday when I took you to our first father-daughter dance," her dad said as they glided across the floor. "You were such a tiny thing."

"I couldn't quite get the two-step, so you let me stand on your shoes." He'd always been her champion.

"I didn't mind one bit." His voice sounded a little choked. "It's nice having you home."

"We text and FaceTime."

"I know." He shrugged. "Bet you're ready to have the school year over. How many more days?"

"Seventeen." Her first graders were getting antsy.

"But who's counting?" He spun her and she bumped into an older couple.

"Sorry," she said to them. "You did that on purpose."

"Who, me?" he chuckled.

She gave him a mock slap on his shoulder and noticed her mother at the side of the room standing with her arms folded. "Spin me again."

"You've got it."

This time she deliberately smiled in her mom's direction. Even from across the room, she could see Mother's glower. But she didn't care, not when the layers of her silky gown swirled like a whirlwind. Whoever thought there'd be advantages to ruffles? "This is fun," she laughed as they danced past Garrett and Josie.

"Yes, it is, shortstop."

Hearing the nickname warmed her heart. "Wish Granny could have made it today." Her adventurous grandmother, Carol Kellogg, was the complete opposite of her mother.

"Me, too."

"I spoke with her this morning. She's furious about having appendix surgery." Granny had always been her rock. She never complained about Birdie being a tomboy, just told her to embrace life.

The song ended. "Thanks for the dance," he said.

"Anytime."

"I'm gonna go find your mom. Promise me another dance later."

"You've got it." She watched her dad stride away.

A waiter walked by. She snatched a champagne glass off the tray, downed the drink, and set it on a table.

Zack moved next to her. "Want another?" He waved the

waiter over and grabbed two glasses and handed them to her. "Drink up."

"You trying to get me drunk?"

"Maybe?"

She had finished off one glass when the band played "Knockin' Boots." Her toes started tapping.

"Dance?" A quick lift of his brow and her pulse whirled through her.

"Sure." She set down her glass, seized his hand and led him to the empty spot not far from the bar. A current of heat shimmied where his hand clasped with hers.

He set one hand on her waist, the other on her shoulder, and they were off two-stepping. She breathed in his masculine scent, noted his broad shoulders, and gazed into his whiskey-colored eyes with flecks of gold flittering through them. He lowered his hand to her waist and brought her a little closer. She wasn't complaining. Not one bit.

He gently tilted her backwards and dipped her. Her left leg went out straight. She kept her balance by hugging his shoulders, reveling in the strength of him. For a second, the world seemed to stop, and they were the only two people in the room. His mouth mere inches away swooped in to capture her lips.

Right there in the middle of all the dancing.

His tongue delved in, deepening the kiss with slow languid swirls. It was as if a flame melted her core, the heat so intense she'd swear he'd ignited her soul.

Then his delicious, warm lips were gone leaving her

starving for more as the tension continued to vibrate through her body.

"I've been dying to do that," his voice came out breathy as he held her in his arms, and they were two-stepping again.

Her knees were weak, her legs wobbly but she somehow managed to hang on. Out of the corner of her eye she caught her mother laughing.

She let out a sigh.

Kissing Zack in the middle of a crowded dance floor wasn't the proper thing to do.

Garrett and Josie glided past them. He gave Zack a thumbs up.

The song changed to the fast beat line dance "Country Girl." Kristy bumped into her. "Hey."

Mia ended up on the other side. "Kinda reminds me of our high school dances."

"Good times." Kristy added while sashaying forward.

"If you like smelly gyms and crepe paper." Birdie laughed. "Although, I do remember having a blast."

And somewhere in the process, she and Zack were dancing with each other again.

Several songs later, Birdie held onto Zack's waist as she moved in a conga line. She spotted her father standing at the side. "Come on, Dad. Join in."

He jogged to her and put his hands on her shoulders. The group snaked forward with a one, two, three, kick momentum. "Enjoying yourself?" he asked.

"I am." Her father had such a chipper, easy going personality. Whenever she was around him, he had this way of making her feel special.

Eyeing the left side of the reception area, she spotted her mom holding her toddler grandson. Her face appeared calm, serene, happy. But the glint in her eyes as she watched them dance said Mother was miffed. No doubt at Birdie. After all, she never did anything right. And the fact she got Dad to join in probably irritated her.

When the song ended, her dad hugged her. "That was great."

"Yes, it was."

"It's time for the couple to cut the cake," the announcer said.

Zack took her hand and weaved her through the crowd to her seat at the long table.

Kristy plunked into the place next to her. "What a reception! You and Zack seem to be hitting it off."

"He's a great dancer."

"And kisser? I saw him sweep you off your feet."

The kiss had been a wonderful surprise, but Birdie didn't want to make a big deal about it. "How's it going with Clint?"

"I really like him."

"I've heard that one before." Her friend tended to fall fast.

"It's different with him."

"I hope so."

Across the room Josie delicately fed Garrett a piece of cake.

"Really?" Birdie whined. "I was hoping to see frosting all over my brother's face."

"I guess that's not Josie's style. She's a bit old-fashioned."

"Why would you say that?"

"She's a little different but in a good way. Garrett's crazy about her."

"Which is all that matters. I'm glad to see him happy. He went through a rough patch after he broke his hand." Her brother had a professional baseball career mapped out before he got hurt.

"Look at him now. Ever the gentleman," Kristy said.

"Are you sure you're talking about my brother?"

"He's a good guy and you know it." Another song played and Kristy got up. Clint waited for her at the edge of the dance floor.

Zack strolled behind her and whispered in her ear. "Let's get a drink." He led her to the bar. "What'll it be?"

"Lemon drop martini. I'll be right back." She needed to use the restroom.

"I'll wait for you right here."

"Sounds good." She stepped outside.

"We need to talk," her mother snarled from right behind her.

"Later, I promise," she didn't slow, focusing on the boxy building with *women* painted on the door.

"Do you thrive on embarrassing your family?" Mother's voice sounded shrill.

Her stomach tightened as she went inside the bathroom.

"Not only are you making a fool of yourself drinking and cavorting with that boy, but did you have to add your father in the mix?"

"Dad's having a great time." No way would she allow this to sour her mood.

Her mom huffed.

An older woman came in. "What a lovely wedding!"

"Thank you." Of course, Mother plastered on her brightest smile.

Birdie went into the stall and shut the door.

"I'll see you inside, sweetie," her mom's voice came out cheerful, but Birdie knew she was masking her anger. Appearances must be maintained.

Nothing ever changes with Mommy Dearest.

CHAPTER 4

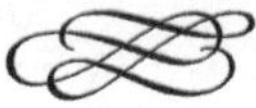

Birdie met up with Zack near the back of the room. She downed her martini as people danced to a twangy country song.

"Thirsty, huh," Zack finished his beer and set it down.

"You don't know the half of it." At least the buzz helped douse some of the exasperation with her mother.

"Wanna get out of here?"

"Definitely."

Zack held her hand as he edged her toward the rear exit. A case of champagne sat on a stand in the corner. She snagged a bottle.

"Garrett never mentioned you could be so sneaky."

"I prefer resourceful."

He let out a chuckle. "Works for me."

They snuck out through the airy opening, past the

wedding arches, rushed down a hill where half a dozen horses were tied to a hitching post, and hurried toward the dirt lot lined with cars.

"I'm parked in the third row. The red Mustang."

She snickered. "A cowboy and his horse."

"I like this car. It's a classic." He opened the door for her.

"Nothing wrong with that. I drive a Challenger."

"V-6 or 8?" He shut her door and got in on the driver's side, setting the bottle in the back seat.

"8, of course."

"Impressive."

"It gets the job done. My parents gave it to me when I graduated from high school." Actually, she'd pleaded with her dad saying since it's all wheel drive the vehicle would make it a great car for rain or snow. Much to mother's dismay. She thought Birdie should get something boring like a Volvo.

"Lucky you." He started up the car. "Where to?"

"What do you suggest?" She rolled down her window. The D.J. played the "Chicken Dance."

"We could find a quiet spot farther north along the river."

"Okay, but first I'd like to change at the farmhouse." Since Granny had been away, she had the place to herself.

"You've got it."

A few minutes later, he pulled in front of the old house with a wrap-around porch.

"Want to come in?" she asked.

"I'll wait here."

She ran inside to the guestroom and practically flung her high-heeled sandals across the room. Then she battled the zipper at the back of her stupid dress, finally got it to cooperate, and threw the pink ruffly ball on a chair in the corner. She quickly donned jeans, a purple blouse and flip-flops. It took several minutes to brush her teeth and take her hair down from the chignon at the back of her neck. Adding a swipe of mascara and a brush of lipstick, she smacked her lips together, snatched her purse and checked the wall clock. Half past nine.

She was back in Zack's car. Kicking up her heels with him made the day entertaining. Life was good.

He turned onto Buckshot Road. Stars blanketed the sky. "I love this time of night."

"So do I." He took a dirt road heading west that meandered along the river, stopping in front of a grassy knoll. "Is this place okay?"

"It's perfect." She got out and breathed in the mixture of wildflowers, grass, and clover. Water lapped along the shore of the Majestic River. Soothing and constant.

Zack threw his suit jacket into the backseat and grabbed the bottle. He opened the trunk, nabbed a red plaid blanket, and spread it on the ground.

She helped smooth out the center. "Let me guess, you're always prepared."

"I do my best." He popped the cork. The green glass sparkled in the moonlight. "I don't have any cups."

"Sharing's fine." She snatched it out of his hand and took

a sip. Bubbles tickled down her throat, making her feel a tinge lightheaded. "Your turn."

He drank a long swig and set the champagne down. "This is nice."

"I know."

His mouth tipped up with an endearing grin. "What made you move hundreds of miles away from here?"

"I like adventure." She reached for the bottle. "As I said, there's plenty to do where I live. Lakes, rivers, parks all within an hour's drive. Since it's a college town, we must have at least twenty night clubs and bars to choose from. The area is so much greener than here because of all the rain and snow."

"Even in the moonlight your eyes light up when you talk about Colorado." He held her hand.

"I love it there."

"It shows. Garrett said you're a teacher. Do you like your job?"

"Very much. First graders are quite active, but they're also little sponges. Most days are enjoyable." She figured she'd found her calling.

"Don't you miss living close to your family?"

"I'm not that far." But far enough away to not have her mom meddling in her business. "A little over two hours with a direct flight. Enough about me." Reaching for the champagne, she took a swig. "Who's your favorite cartoon character?"

"Mickey Mouse."

"Really. You're telling me you like rodents," she spoke imitating the character's high squeaky voice.

He laughed. "Just Mickey. After all, he is the ambassador for Disneyland. I bet you like all of the princesses."

"Nope. Bugs Bunny. He loves creating mischief and chaos."

"Daffy's better."

"You're wrong." She said in a duck voice. "Bugs always outsmarts Daffy. Remember the episode when they argued over duck season and rabbit season. Bugs kept tricking him into saying, 'Duck season.'"

"I still prefer Daffy."

"Then I guess we'll have to agree to disagree." She liked bantering with him. "What about video games?"

"Mostly racing or sports. You?"

"I hate to admit I'm addicted to Bejeweled. Once I was playing it in the airport and almost missed my connecting flight. Still, when I have time, I'd rather be outside."

"I'm the same way."

His index finger pressed under her chin, tipping her face up to look directly at him. Those devastating eyes had every cell in her body buzzing with awareness.

Gently sucking her lower lip, he kissed her with a slow, lazy sweep of his tongue. Joining in, she melded with him and got lost in his mouth. Savoring the warmth and taste of champagne. He matched her kiss for kiss. Her lungs were starved for oxygen, but they kept on. Hot and heavy. He slipped his arm around her waist tugging her closer.

A helicopter flew over them, and they broke apart.

"I'd better take you home."

"Okay." His action was sensible, even though a part of her wanted to stay longer. She brought her mouth to his for one long leisurely kiss.

And then they packed up and left.

ZACK PARKED in front of the old farmhouse. He liked the place because it reminded him of the home where he grew up. He still couldn't believe his luck getting time alone with this beauty and hoped she'd invite him inside again.

She got out before he had a chance to open the door for her.

Did she know a gentleman opens a door for a lady? He followed her up the steps. "I had fun." He pressed her against the door, lowered his head and brushed his lips against hers and kissed her. "I'd like to see you again before you leave." He wasn't quite ready to end this evening.

"I wish I could. I'm busy all day tomorrow."

Damn.

He said the first thing that came to his mind. "Have a safe trip home."

"I will." She went inside, leaving him longing for more.

After spending time with her, he liked her. She was sweet and full of fun. Still, her departure was for the best since he had a secret he preferred not to share.

CHAPTER 5

The next morning, Birdie stretched her arms and opened her eyes. Light filtered in from the windows. She fingered the gray and white striped sheets. Not silky and pastel yellow like in her own bed.

The old Singer sewing machine sat in the corner. On shelves above it, she spotted neatly folded fabric, spools of thread in varying colors, and a large wicker sewing basket. As a kid, Birdie was certain the basket must be magical because of the bobbins, zippers, needles, patches, and hundreds of buttons. One time, Granny pulled out a handmade felt dog complete with a big snout and tongue that hung out, large wiggle eyes, and floppy black ears. In her opinion, Granny was way better than Mary Poppins.

She'd kept her stuffed animal named Muffin over the

years. Unfortunately, when she moved out of the dorms in college, the dog got lost. But not the memories.

Too bad Granny hadn't made it to the wedding. If she were here, Birdie would have woken up to the smell of freshly baked cinnamon rolls or maybe homemade donuts. Her mouth watered remembering those tasty treats.

Another time. The farmhouse wasn't going anywhere.

She got up and gazed into the oval mirror above the dresser. Her lips were puffier than usual, and she thought about Zack's marvelous kisses. She wouldn't mind a repeat performance. Too bad she was leaving tonight.

What time was it anyway? She reached for her phone.

11:26.

That late. In a little over an hour, she was expected at her older brother's house. She loved being with her niece and nephew whenever she was in town but also wished she could borrow one of the ranch's horses. Her busy schedule today made riding out of the question.

First there was Tyler's. Then dinner at her parent's house with the whole gang—minus the newlyweds off on their honeymoon. If she were lucky, she'd be seated by Uncle Al. He was always good for a laugh.

After showering and dressing in jeans and a T-shirt, she headed into the kitchen and plopped a hazelnut flavored coffee pod into the Keurig machine. She looked out the window in the direction of Fairfield Farms and wondered what Zack might be doing. She regretted not having more time to spend with him.

Her phone rang, and she plucked it off the nightstand. "Hey, Kris. How was your night?"

"Wonderful. Clint brought me to a cove on the other side of the river and … well … I really like him." She gave a wistful sound. "He's taking me to a concert next Saturday."

"That's great." She grabbed a cup, added cream, a spoonful of sugar, and stirred. The nutty coffee aroma filled her nostrils. "Where does Clint live?"

"Whiskeyville."

"That's not far. Since he was at the wedding, I assume he knows Garrett or Josie?"

"Garrett played with him on a traveling baseball team in junior high."

"I kind of remember that name, but to be honest, Mom had continually dragged me to pageants, so I rarely got to watch Garrett play."

"I remember how much you hated competing," Kristy agreed. "So … what happened with you and Zack."

"Not much to tell. We went to a spot near the river and drank champagne. He's great, but I'm going home. We'd be fools to think a long-distance relationship would work." But boy was she tempted.

"You can say that again." Kristy's high school sweetheart moved to the East Coast for college and he met someone else. "When do we need to head for the airport?"

"My flight doesn't leave until eleven. Eight should be fine. That'll give me an hour to get there and plenty of time to get through security. Or you could rescue me at seven and we'll stop for a drink." She wouldn't mind cutting out early from the family dinner.

"Seven it is. I wish you were staying longer."

"Me, too." After last night with Zack, she wouldn't mind another day. "But this is a bad time of year for me. I've got tons of student assessments to complete, and then report cards and comments all due in seven days."

"Coming from the girl who finished her term paper ten minutes before it was due and still got an A."

"If you'll remember, doing five term papers that quarter about killed me."

CHAPTER 6

The front door slammed, and Kristy set a bag from In-N-Out Burger on the countertop. She took out two cans of soda from the refrigerator.

"You're the best." Zack pulled out a barstool and sat.

"Flattery will get you everywhere." She wore a beaming smile as she handed him a burger and fries.

"How was work?" He pulled off a fry covered with cheese, caramelized onions, and special sauce, and savored the delicious flavor.

"Great. Actually, someone told me about this genealogy website that's supposed to have lots of info. Are you ready to do a search?"

When he first arrived to this century, he hadn't been eager to research his family. The thought that he'd been with them one day and in a few hours, they were all gone. Dead.

And had been dead for over a hundred years. He couldn't wrap his head around all that happened.

Kristy hadn't pushed the issue. But he was now okay with it. Every day he missed his siblings. All nine of them. Missed his parents, aunts and uncles.

"Let's finish eating and I'll pull up the site."

"Sounds good to me." He ate his burger quickly ready to delve into his past.

"I'm curious to see what happened."

"They all died," he said in a deadpan tone.

"Well, duh." Kristy did a crazy sign with her finger. She tapped on her tablet's keyboard. "Harris with two 'r's and one 's', right?"

"Yep." Hearing his real name sounded odd. Her parents suggested Zack take their surname of Fairfield when he'd arrived at the ranch. For the past three years he'd gotten used to acting as their kin. It made for a lot fewer questions.

"What was your dad's name?"

"Charles."

Her fingers glided over the keyboard. "The top hit is from 1880. The location New York."

"That won't work."

"No worries. There's plenty more." Her eyes were glued to the screen. "Bingo. The census is from 1870. It shows Charles' wife as Mary Harrison and lists you and what must be your siblings." She handed him her tablet.

He smiled as he read the names, Cora, Eric, Ida, Zack, and John. "This is incredible."

"Right?"

"But it doesn't tell me what happened to them." He sank back into the couch.

"See if there's a tab on the side or bottom for that."

"Got it. Pa lived from 1842 to 1901." He counted on his fingers. "That would make him close to sixty when he died." The idea made him happy.

"That's old for the century. I think I read the average life expectancy was around 35." She scrunched up her nose. "Wait. That could be me in ten years."

"And me. Life was harder back then. People worked long hours."

"So do people in this century."

"Good point. At least medicine is better now. Remember when I cut my hand and it got infected." His hand swelled to twice its size. "Those tablets of penicillin cured it pretty quickly. In my time, a guy could lose a limb or even die from that."

"I tend to take things for granted."

"It's easy to do."

She smiled at him. "I'm so glad I happened to find you. You fit in well here."

"You and your family make it easy." They treated him like he belonged.

"We try. Enough with the mushy talk and back to the website." She had tears in her eyes. "Is there anything about your mom? See if there's any links on your dad's page near the bottom."

"I found it." He clicked on the tab. "Oh, shit"

"What's wrong?"

"Ma died on March 1, 1888." His stomach squeezed like it was inside a vice. "Six months after I left."

"I'm so sorry." She moved to his side and hugged him. "Do you remember her being ill?"

"She had bouts of coughing, but I had no idea she was that bad."

"It could have been tuberculosis. The disease was prevalent then."

"What's that?"

"A lung disease." She snagged her tablet and typed. "It used to be called consumption."

"When I was about twelve, my friend's dad died of consumption. I remembered the man coughing up blood." The room got really hot, and he struggled to suck in air. He couldn't imagine his dear, sweet mother, the woman who managed to win a blue ribbon at the county fair for her peach cobbler while keeping him and his siblings in line, had her life cut short by a disease that was rare in this century."

During his last conversation with her, he'd said some terse words when she made him clean out the pig stye the morning before he left. Mind you, his dad and other brothers were out branding, and the job needed to be done, still he'd been agitated. After bathing in the river, he'd been running late and didn't even say goodbye before he left. He'd never told Ma how much he loved and appreciated her. "I should have been there." He'd left to help with a cattle run on his aunt and uncle's ranch, but he was supposed to return in October. Well before Ma died."

"You didn't choose to leave."

"Maybe not, but after learning Garrett could go back, I could have attempted to get back to her."

"Time travel doesn't always work. Anyway, I'm glad you're here."

"Thanks. If you and your family hadn't taken me in, I don't know how I'd survive." He was just a visitor to this century.

"Given your brawn and brains, you would do just fine." Kristy got up and hugged him.

"You like me for my muscles." He flexed his biceps.

She laughed. "Plus, you make a great roommate. If you weren't around, I'd have to eat both those burgers. You've saved me from myself." She punched him in the arm.

"Glad to be of service." He liked living in modern times. Liked hot showers, fast food, and hot rods. Liked his friends.

"You're exactly where you belong."

He hugged her tight, appreciating of her support.

But … a part of him longed to see his family.

CHAPTER 7

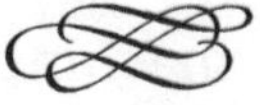

Her first day of summer break, Birdie had packed up her car ready to spend the weekend water skiing. Thinking only of herself and the fun she'd have.

Until Dad called. "*Your grandmother had a heart attack.*"

Her pulse sped through her veins faster than a starship on hyperdrive. Heart attacks can be deadly.

Granny couldn't die. Not her rock, her pillar of reason, the dearest woman in her world.

Since no seats were open on any flights until later the next night, she opted to drive.

After ten hours on the road her butt hurt. Her shoulders ached. Her legs cramped. Worry had her clutching the steering wheel so hard her knuckles throbbed. At close to midnight, she pulled into a rest stop in the middle of Nowhere Nevada to stretch.

Headlights flashed through the windshield of her Challenger. Blinking, it took her several seconds to get her bearings.

Another four or five hours and she'd be in Surprise Valley.

It took her five minutes to use the restroom and grab a coffee from the vending machine. She needed caffeine to keep alert.

Back on the interstate, her phone rang. She pushed accept on the car's screen. "Hey, Dad."

"Your grandmother ended up with a triple bypass. Don't worry. Everything went well. She's resting now."

Her eyes teared up as she said a silent prayer of thanks. Granny would be all right. "That's great. How soon will you be able to see her?"

"Not for an hour or two."

She glanced at the time on the dashboard. 11 p.m. "You must be exhausted."

"I am. I sent your mother home. Tyler and Garrett are still inside."

"Did you get ahold of Henry?" Her youngest brother was studying abroad for the summer in Germany.

"Yes." Her dad gave a weary sigh.

"That's great. I should be there by five." She needed to see Granny as soon as possible.

"Please drive safely. I know how you love to speed," he laughed.

"Don't worry, Dad. I'll be fine." Leave it to her father to

pick up her spirits.

TEN HOURS LATER, Birdie sat by her grandmother in the hospital room. She was attached to countless tubes and plugs and apparatuses. A heart rate monitor beeped. A blood pressure cuff inflated around her arm and made an annoying noise. 98/76 flashed on the screen. Was that good?

A tear dripped down her cheek.

"Granny, I need you more than you'll ever know." She reached for her hand and squeezed it.

"Birdie?" a hoarse voice spoke. Paper-thin eyelids opened and attempted to focus on her.

"It's me."

"Oh, honey, you didn't have to come all this way."

Typical Granny, recovering in the ICU from heart surgery and more concerned for Birdie. Carol Kellogg was tough. She'd survived. She had to. "How you feeling?"

"Sleepy." Granny yawned and closed her eyes.

"Hey, shortstop," her dad walked in. "You look worn out. Go home and get some sleep. I'll stay with her."

"I'll be back early tomorrow." Pretty much dead on her feet, she walked out into the waiting room and spotted her mother sitting ramrod stiff in one of the chairs. "Hi."

"I'm glad you came," her mom said so softly Birdie thought she might have imagined the words.

"Thanks." She kissed her cheek and hurried to the glass

doors and on to the outside world, letting out the breath she didn't know she'd been holding. Granny would be okay.

CHAPTER 8

Birdie arrived in town about a week ago, but Zack hadn't run into the cute dynamo yet.

Eight o'clock on a Saturday night, he strolled into the saloon. Tables were filled with people and the place hopped. He sat at the bar and motioned to Clint for a beer. "Is Kristy here yet?" They'd been dating since Garrett's wedding.

"Over there." Clint pointed.

Scores of women line-danced to some twangy country song on a rectangular floor. Kristy stood dead-center, wearing a pink Stetson and a shit-eating grin. His eyes drifted to the right and his heart skidded to a stop.

Birdie.

The honey-haired beauty sauntered forward and then hitched her leg back to the "Moose Knuckle Shuffle." Zack's eyes roved over her sweet curves. Then she did a hip bump with John Tucker the best dancer in the whole damn town. He wanted to push the guy aside and take his place.

The song ended. Kristy grabbed her arm, and the pair headed his way.

"Hey, cuz." Kristy slid onto a bar stool.

Birdie moved to his cousin's right and said, "Hello."

"Can I buy you ladies a drink?"

"Lemon Drop Martini," Kristy called out.

"Same for me." Birdie's mouth jerked upward giving him a half-smile.

"When's your grandmother coming home?" Zack asked, hoping for the best.

"Tomorrow afternoon."

Kristy picked up her drink. "To Granny and a speedy recovery."

They clinked their glasses.

He leaned on his elbow. "How long you staying?"

"At least another week or two, maybe longer."

A lively two-step played on the juke box. "Wanna dance?"

Birdie took a sip of her drink and stood. "Sure."

Zack offered his hand. It felt right to have her in his arms. She'd obviously been under a lot of stress and wasn't as bubbly as she had been at the wedding. That night she'd made him feel like he could do anything. He spun her under his arm pleased to see her grin, and his insides twisted a little bit.

She laughed. "This is just what I needed."

"Why is that?"

"I'm used to being busy and lately I've spent far too much time sitting."

"I'm the same way. That's why I like ranching. There's always something to do." He loved how the daily physical labor made his muscles burn.

She ran her hand up his arm and squeezed his biceps. "I can tell."

A zing of electricity seemed to shoot straight to his groin. "Thanks." He thought about saying, *Feel free to touch me whenever you want,* but decided to hold his tongue.

She yawned.

"Am I boring you?"

"Not at all. The last few days have been exhausting. I haven't been getting much sleep."

"That's too bad. Anyway, I'm sure your family appreciates that you're here."

"They do." She looked toward the bar. His cousin was talking with Clint. "I'd better have Kristy take me home."

"I can do it if you'd like."

"If Kristy's not ready to go, that would be great." She headed for her friend.

A few minutes later they were in his car and driving off. Her phone chimed with a text. She glanced at it and frowned.

"Everything okay."

"Just Garrett checking to see if I'll be at the hospital tomorrow morning." Her eyes got misty. "I hate that Granny had a heart attack."

"It must be hard holding it together."

"It ... it is," she gulped, and he could tell she was fighting back tears.

"Granny's gonna make it. That's all that matters."

"I'm trying to be positive but ... she accepts me for me."

"Is there anything I can do to help?" He wanted to be there for her.

"Not really. As I said before, the family will pitch in."

"Of course they will. At least you're not alone."

He turned onto her street and pulled into the driveway in front of the farmhouse. Once stopped, he held her in his arms as she sobbed.

"I'm sorry," she sputtered. "I never cry."

"It's okay, really." He put the car in park, unclipped his seatbelt and wrapped his arm around her.

"No, it's not." She hiccupped. "Crying makes me weak."

"You're not weak, Birdie." He smoothed a strand of hair behind her ear.

She pushed out of his grasp and wiped her face with the back of her hand.

"I'll be right next door if you need me. Give me your phone, and I'll put in my number."

"Here."

"Feel free to call if you need to get out of the house again. We could get coffee or go riding."

"I might take you up on that. You're really nice." She kissed him on the cheek, unsnapped her seatbelt and slid out of the car.

He watched her disappear into the house. If only he could hold her and tell her everything would be all right.

CHAPTER 9

The next morning, Birdie waited in the hospital room with her chair next to Granny. "How you feeling?"

"I'll be a lot better once I get off these blasted machines. The beeping keeps me up all night," Granny grumbled.

"Be patient. The doctor should be releasing you soon. Since we're alone, I've got something to ask you." She bit her bottom lip.

"What's up?"

"Would it be okay with you if I stayed for the whole summer?" Birdie let out a long breath. She decided to change her plans last night.

"It's not necessary. I've got plenty of people who can help me if I need it. Which I probably won't." Granny adjusted her pillow. "You don't need to worry about me."

"As if you'd let a silly heart attack get you down." Birdie

fought off the idea of how serious Granny's condition had been.

"You've got that right. Next year, Myrtle and I have plans to snorkel and paraglide in Hawaii." Granny's eyes lit. "The tickets are nonrefundable."

"I'm sure you two will go, but this is your time with me. We're going to get you better. You'll need some sunshine and a lot of laughter. And I'm just the person to help you with that."

Granny squinted. "What about your Colorado friends? I hate to see you give up everything just to entertain me."

"That's not how I see it. It doesn't matter if we're riding horses or gardening or taking a road trip. I always enjoy myself with you."

"True enough. Remember when we drove up to Solvang."

"I love that Dutch community near Santa Barbara. The shops are so cute."

"They sure are. You must've been about eight when I took you."

"Seven. You let me wear my red-striped shorts with that tie-dyed multicolored T-shirt and Gramps fishing hat. I knew even then my outfit was over the top, but you never said a word."

"I thought you looked precious." Granny took her hand. "We must have gone into every souvenir shop."

"I remember you bought Gramps a hunting knife with a fancy leather case."

"And you finished one Danish and asked for another

which you saved for the drive home. When we got outside you twirled like the blades on the windmill."

"And you danced with me."

"Why wouldn't I?"

Yep, Granny always understood her.

"Still, your older now. Wouldn't you rather hang out with people your own age?"

"No Granny, this is you and I having adventures. And while I'm in town, I can hang out with Kristy and Mia."

"And there's that nice friend of Garrett's. I heard all about the spectacle you made of yourself." Granny winked. "From the story your mom told me, you showed sass. Reminds me of myself at that age."

Birdie didn't want to think about Zack right now. "Speaking of Mother, that's another reason you need me around. You know she'll wanna barge right in and start bullying you to do this and that."

Granny's brow furrowed. "Not if I have a say in things."

"Then indulge me. We'll have the best summer ever."

"You drive a hard bargain." Granny shook her hand.

"Don't you know it. Think about the fun we're gonna have." Birdie rubbed her hands together. "Just remember, you'll need to take things slow for a few weeks, maybe more."

"What ideas do you have for week three?"

"You're too much."

"That's why you love me." Her lips trembled into a wobbly grin.

"You're easy to love. Anyway, as for our plans, we'll do

something calm. Maybe take a train down to the beach or rent a cabin up in Big Bear." Birdie paused for a second. "That is, after your doctor gives his okay."

"He will. It's too bad your parents' beach house is getting remodeled. That place would be perfect."

"Probably couldn't have got it anyway." Mother inherited the place and rented it out whenever she could. She liked getting the extra money. "Don't worry. We'll figure something out."

"With you in charge I have no doubt."

"I'm surprised you trust me. You used to call me a wild child."

"The word is hellion." Granny let out a loud guffaw. "And you wear it well."

Birdie burst in a fit of giggles.

"What are you two talking about?" Her mom rushed in. "I could hear you from the nurses' desk." She glared at Birdie.

"Reminiscing along with a little laughing. It's good for my heart." Granny smirked at Birdie.

"The doctor just signed the release papers. Ready to get out of here?" Dad walked in smiling.

"More than you'll ever know."

CHAPTER 10

After getting Granny settled on the couch, her mom set the thermostat up from seventy-six to seventy-nine insisting the place was too cold. Mind you, the hospital room had stayed a steady seventy degrees, but Mother always knew what was best. Dad chatted with Granny and didn't once glance up to his wife.

Birdie snagged a bottle of water from the fridge.

"Your dress is wrinkled." What she really meant was Birdie's outfit didn't meet Mother's personal standards. It wasn't like she hadn't heard that tone before.

"Mom just leave it alone. It's fine." Birdie didn't want to argue right now.

"If you say so, sweetie."

She walked over to Granny, tucking a throw over her legs. "Anything I can get you."

"Just water."

Birdie unscrewed the cap and handed her the bottle.

Granny sat up a little and took a big gulp. "Just what I needed."

Mother's eyes squinted, then she took control of the kitchen and set a pan with salmon in the oven.

"Be a doll, Roberta, and fix the salad."

Birdie washed the vegetables.

"Use the grater on the smaller side. The carrots taste better when they're smaller."

"I'm a twenty-five-year-old woman. I think I know what I'm doing." She snatched a carrot and used the larger end of the grater. Cut three tomatoes into halves, fourths, then eights. Sliced avocadoes. Added the items in a large bowl with arugula lettuce. Poured in vinaigrette dressing and tossed the salad.

Mother set the table for three and took out the fish. "I hope you're hungry."

"Starved." Granny rubbed her stomach. "Hospital food can be pretty bland."

"Need help sitting up?" Dad asked from the chair next to her.

"Please."

A few minutes later, her mom set a plate of salmon with salad in a side bowl on a TV tray in front of Granny.

"I was really hoping Jacob would fire up the barbeque and cook us steaks."

"Can't do it. Remember what the doctor said. You need to

limit your consumption of red meat." Dad patted Granny's shoulder.

"We must control your fat intake, so fish is the best option. It's vital for your recovery. I'll be coming by every day to make sure you have proper meals." Mother had that I-know-what's-best-for-you look.

Birdie straightened her shoulders. "I'll be here for the summer."

"But … well … I don't mean to sound ungrateful for my daughter's sacrifice, but she isn't … much of a cook," Mother sputtered.

"That's not true. Last year when I visited her in Colorado, she made some incredible meals during my stay. You'll have to try her chicken tortilla soup and spinach salad sometime." Granny smirked. "I'm just tickled to spend some time with my granddaughter."

"What a marvelous plan. It will be nice to have you home for more than a few days." Her father gave her a broad smile.

"Thanks, Dad." Birdie grabbed a plate and went to the overstuffed chair next to Granny and tucked her feet underneath her.

Dad picked up a plate off the table, filled it with food and took the recliner.

"The table's set, Jacob. Come join me."

"I'd rather stay by Mom." His lips quirked up on one side.

"Fine." To the average eye, Mother appeared composed except that her lips pinched together, and her cheeks flushed to a shade of dark pink. Yep, Mother was miffed. She moved to the table set for three—all alone.

Birdie expected her mom to fight this issue but she probably backed down because of Granny's condition.

Not about to miss a game Dad clicked on the TV remote to baseball. "The Red Wings are playing. Bases are loaded."

"Johnson's up to bat," Birdie rubbed her hands together.

"He's batting 297 and due for a homerun. Come on Teddy," Granny chanted.

The batter swung and the bat clinked with the ball.

"It's over the fence." Dad stood. "Unbelievable."

"Gramps must be whooping it up in heaven." Granny gave a faraway look. "I miss that old coot."

"So do I," Birdie joined in. "Do you still have his lucky cap? That thing was gross."

"It was. He refused to wash it even when he dropped it in one of the stalls he'd been mucking out." Granny scrunched her nose. "But after he passed, I couldn't part with it. I put the thing up in the attic if you want it."

"Maybe later," Birdie glanced at Mother.

She arched a brow and went back to eating.

Birdie finished her food and got up. "Can I get you anything, Granny? Dad?"

"Nothing. Could you take this?" Dad passed her his plate.

"I'm done, too," Granny said.

As Birdie moved closer to Granny, her face appeared wane and rather chalky. Had she overdone it today? Birdie chewed her bottom lip. Granny was strong. She'd be fine. She had to be fine.

"You should lie down. Want me to help you to your bed?" her mother said.

"I'm perfectly okay on the couch."

A scowl flitted across her mom's face but was quickly replaced by a phony smile.

Dad fluffed Granny's pillow and helped her get settled.

Birdie rinsed off the dishes and put them in the dishwasher.

Someone knocked on the door.

"I'll get it. It's your brother."

"Hey." Garrett walked in with Josie.

"Join me at the table." Whenever her brother walked into a room, Mother's eyes lit up like it was Christmas. "There's plenty of food if you're hungry."

"In a minute." Garrett kneeled in front of Granny. "I bet you're glad to be home."

"Don't you know it." She patted his hand. "Now you two go get some food. I'm not going anywhere."

Garrett kissed her cheek.

An hour later, her parents were gone, leaving Birdie alone with Granny, Garrett, and Josie.

"That was exhausting." Granny murmured. "Jacob and Laura mean well, but …"

Garrett motioned to Birdie. "Try growing up with them."

"Dad's not bad. But Mother ..." Birdie shook her head.

"I'm going to bed. You guys enjoy yourselves." Granny managed to stand but not without a little whimper.

Garrett walked her into her bedroom.

Josie opened the fridge and snagged a soda. "Want one?"

"Sure."

"She's gonna be okay."

"I know." Still, a speck of worry couldn't help sneaking its way into her brain.

"She's already asleep," Garrett said as he entered the room. "Josie and I will stay for the next few hours. Why don't you call Kristy and get out of here?"

"Okay." Not about to waste this opportunity, she grabbed her phone and went outside on the veranda.

Birdie: *U at work.*

Kristy: *Yep.*

Birdie: *Damn. I need a break from here.*

Kristy: *Zack's home. Ask him.*

Zack had given her his number. Why not?

Birdie: *You free 4 that cup of coffee?*

Zack: *Need to finish chores. B done in about an hour. I can pick you up.*

Birdie: *K.*

CHAPTER 11

Zack parked near the side gate of the farmhouse. Birdie hopped into the mustang. Her legs were bare up to her thigh where the top of her shorts hit. A tank top stretched across her breasts. Her long light brown hair was loose around her shoulders. But what made her sexy as all getup was her emerald eyes that seemed to brighten as she glanced at him.

"Thanks for coming. I really need to unwind. I hate seeing Gran suffer and my mother drives me crazy." She struggled with the seatbelt and finally clicked it in place. "I know I said coffee, but what I'd really like is a hot fudge sundae."

"You've got it." He turned onto the street.

"Tyler said you're working with a spirited stallion. Think he'll take long to break?"

"Probably." Uncle Will purchased the horse on a trip to Utah. "He's a gorgeous bay quarter horse, but it doesn't take much to spook him. A simple sneeze makes him antsy. A car horn has him rearing up and losing his rider."

"Sounds like a challenge."

"Yep. At the very least, he'll make a good stud." Zack drove into the small parking lot. Melting Memories Ice Cream Parlor sat to the left. High Desert Diner in the middle. Surprise Valley Mini-Mart on the right.

He held the door as they entered the shop. The sweet scent reminded him of taffy pulls he'd done at a church picnic. Stretching the sugary candy had been entertaining, especially when his sister dropped her end in the grass. People in this century didn't need to pull taffy when anyone could just as easily buy things from stores like this one. Every time he came here, his thoughts turned to his sister Sophia. He wondered what she would think of this place. They not only sold candy but fifty different ice cream flavors. He imagined the delight on her face at such a huge selection. He shook his head to clear his thoughts and stood next to Birdie at the glass counter. "You still want a sundae?"

"Yes, but I'd like to add a brownie on the bottom, a scoop of chocolate chip, hot fudge, whipped cream, and three cherries," her voice came out bubbly.

"Good choice," the teenage girl behind the counter said. She must be new because he didn't remember her working here. "What would you like?"

"A double butter pecan cone. Both on my bill." He handed over his debit card.

"I can pay."

"It's my treat." As far as he was concerned, these newfangled dating ideas in the twenty-first century were foolish. The man should get the bill.

"Thanks." She snagged her sundae from the counter, immediately spooned a bite, and hummed. "This is yummy." A little dab of whip cream remained in the corner of her mouth.

He had a sudden impulse to lick it off but decided not to act.

They walked past self-service bins filled with jellybeans, taffy, licorice in a rainbow of colors, and chocolates.

"Remind me to get some strawberry licorice before I leave. It's Granny's favorite."

"Is that your favorite, too?"

"It's good, but I'd rather have a Snickers. What about you?"

"I'm a Skittles guy."

"What's your favorite color?"

"If I had to pick one, it's orange." He gave her a flirty smile. "But I like them all." In his time, his choices were restricted to lollipops, caramels, taffy, gum drops, and lemon drops

"I don't care for the purple ones. I mean, they're supposed to be grape, but they just taste weird."

"Not to me."

She took a bite of her sundae and flicked her tongue along her top lip. "Penny for your thoughts?"

"Just thinking about how pretty you are."

"Thanks." Her cheeks turned into a soft pink.

A song about a man and his horse twanged from the speakers in the wall. "Now that your grandma's doing okay, you leaving soon?"

"I've decided to stay for the summer."

Yes. She'd be here for two months. He wanted to throw his hat in the air and shout *yippee* but stifled his elation. This would give him a chance to spend more time with her and hopefully turn their friendship into something more. "Then I'd like to take you out sometime."

"I'm kinda taking things day by day."

"I get it. What if I check back with you on Friday?"

"Perfect." Her eyes twinkled.

BIRDIE STROLLED INSIDE and caught Garrett making out with his wife on the couch and cleared her throat.

The two broke apart.

"How's Kristy?" Josie asked. "We were supposed to go out for lunch last week, but she ended up doing a double shift."

"She's trying to earn extra cash."

"Was that Zack's car I heard?" Garrett peered at her.

"Can't get anything past you. Kristy was working and suggested I give Zack a call. We went out for ice cream."

She couldn't help grinning. Zack had been excellent company.

"And you didn't bring me back any rocky road? I thought I was your favorite brother." His mouth turned down into a mock frown.

"I've been craving cherries jubilee. Maybe we could stop by the ice cream shop before we head home." She patted her baby bump.

"Of course." He kissed Josie's cheek. The gesture was sweet and a change from the brother she grew up with.

"How's Granny doing?"

"We were talking about Zack." Garrett shook his head.

"Actually, we were talking about ice cream."

"She's got a point." Josie giggled. "Granny's sleeping. I think the day got to her."

"Good. Why don't you two head out?"

"Okay. Remember if you need anything, I'm only a phone call away." He got up and hugged Birdie. "I've always got your back."

Of all her brothers, Garrett and she were the closest probably because they were only a little over a year apart.

"Appreciate it." She squeezed him a little harder and let go.

"When Granny's better we should have a girl's luncheon. I'm sure Kristy, Mia, and April would love it."

"Great idea." Birdie hugged Josie. She really was nice.

The pair walked out. Birdie found Granny's bedroom

door open and peeked inside. Needing to be certain she was breathing, she walked into the room.

"You have a good time?" Granny's voice boomed.

Birdie startled. "You scared me."

"Sorry, honey. Come sit with me and talk." Granny let out a long breath. "How's Zack? He's a nice man."

"We went out for ice cream." Birdie sat at the foot of the bed.

Granny's face was a bit gaunt, although the color was much better than it had been in the hospital. "I'm glad to see you and Zack are friends. I like him."

"Me, too."

"You and I are a lot alike. We both crave adventure. It's driving me crazy that I have to slow down." Granny folded her arms. "Just promise you won't treat me like an invalid."

"I won't hover, but that doesn't mean I won't expect you to take it easy. The last thing I want is for you to go back in the hospital."

"Neither do I. Remember if you get bored, you don't have to stick around. This is your summer vacation."

"I'd do anything for you, Granny." She meant every word. "I was so scared when I heard about …"

Granny hugged her. "I'm fine."

"Well, in a week or two we could drive to Wrightwood for lunch. After that, maybe a weekend in Palm Springs."

Granny's face lit with happiness. "Remember that karaoke bar we visited there? You ended up with a standing ovation with your rendition of Jolene."

"Didn't Mia and Kristy join us for that trip?"

"They did along with my friend Myrtle." Granny's eyes glinted. "What we need is a girls' weekend."

"Definitely. We'll plan something for after the Fourth of July."

"If I can wait that long." Granny yawned.

Birdie got up and kissed her cheek. "Get some sleep."

CHAPTER 12

Three days later, Granny answered the front door.

"For you, Mrs. K."

Birdie recognized that deep baritone voice. Zack had texted earlier to see if Granny was up for a visit. He also asked her to go horseback riding afterwards.

"How did you know yellow roses are my favorite, Zack?" She ushered him inside.

"A little birdie told me." He gazed at Birdie with amusement.

She couldn't help but smile. Zack really was a good guy.

"Of course she did." Granny went into the kitchen and put the flowers in a vase. "How 'bout a glass of lemonade?"

"Sure."

"Have a seat." Birdie motioned him to the couch. "I'll get it." She hopped up, not about to have Granny carry anything heavy. Seconds later, she set down a tray with drinks and a plate of cookies on the coffee table and took the empty seat on Zack's right.

Granny snagged two cookies and eased into a recliner.

Zack sipped his lemonade. "This is really good, Mrs. K."

"Thanks. Birdie picked the lemons for me."

"What are your plans for this afternoon?" Zack asked her grandmother.

"Thought I might start training for a triathlon. Need to increase my cycling speed."

Birdie burst out laughing. Only Granny would come up with a line like that.

"Darn it. I left my bicycle at home," Zack spoke with a chuckle.

"That's okay. Birdie told me you and her are going for a ride."

"We'll be gone for an hour or two." Zack gave a disarming smile, and Birdie found her body getting warmer. "But if you need her, we can do that another time."

"Not at all. A couple of my friends are coming over for bunko. I plan to win every pot." Granny winked. "You two have fun."

"Thanks again for the lemonade and cookies." He got up, collected the glasses, and brought the tray into the kitchen.

She couldn't help watching his backside as he walked away.

~

RIDING TURNED out to be just what Birdie needed. The speed. The wind in her hair. The thunder of horse's hoofs pounding the ground. The sense that only she, Zack, and nature existed as they galloped along the wash created by a flashflood centuries ago. "Race you to the water tower."

His stallion edged past Buttercup. "I won," he shouted when he reached the tower and slowed his mount.

"That's because you're on that stallion." She took off her Stetson and fanned her face. "The odds were in your favor."

His eyes crinkled. "It was a close race." They turned their horses and headed back to the farmhouse.

"How did you know I could ride? I might be like my cousin, Mia. She's terrified of horses." An inexperienced rider with the wrong horse could spell disaster.

"First off, Garrett told me you're a skilled rider. And ever since Mia met Dusty, she's been learning to overcome that fear."

"Right. I forgot her husband has been teaching her." Mia had mentioned this on the phone a while ago. Two years ago when Birdie came to California, her cousin had been drawn to a cowboy photo in an antique shop's window. She had talked non-stop about the cowboy who ended up hanging at the turn of the nineteenth century. Shortly after their trip, Mia fell in love with a guy who was a ringer for the guy. Mia had called it fate. Birdie just found the whole thing weird. "Don't you think it's crazy that Mia and Dusty are married? I mean, I'm happy for them, but I could never see myself married."

"You don't imagine getting hitched someday?" He eyed her sideways.

"Not anytime soon." Why would she? "I like the freedom of being single."

"So do I. I enjoyed our ride." He flashed her a smile.

They reached the front of the farmhouse and she dismounted, handing him the reins.

"You're going to Garrett's birthday party on Saturday, right?" he asked.

"Already promised Granny I'd take her."

"Then I'll see you there." She couldn't help skipping into the house. Racing with Zack had been a blast.

CHAPTER 13

The sun glared in Birdie's eyes as she parked her Challenger against the curb behind Zack's candy apple red Mustang. He got out and went around to open the passenger's door for Kristy.

"Zack's here." Birdie found herself smiling.

Granny unbuckled her seatbelt. "That boy reminds me of your grandfather."

Birdie cocked her head and eyed Zack wearing a black T-shirt that accentuated his muscular build. Opening the door, Granny swung her legs out and stood. She had meant to assist her, but her grandmother got out with ease. The way she moved nobody would ever guess she'd had surgery two weeks ago.

Kristy rushed towards Birdie holding a present with

cupcake wrapping paper. A huge grin graced her face. "Ready to roast your brother?"

"You bet." Birdie opened the hatch of her trunk and reached for her brother's gift and grabbed a container of homemade brownies.

Zack strode next to Granny and offered his arm. "May I escort you?"

"I'd be honored." Her grandmother clutched him.

Watching Zack with Granny touched her from deep inside her heart. He really was considerate, which made him even more attractive to her.

One of Kristy's eyebrows lifted. "You know he's interested."

"I'm considering it." Since she broke up with her last boyfriend several months ago, she could use a just-for-now diversion.

Kristy placed a hand on her hip. "Anyway, we've got some partying to do."

She and Kristy headed for her parents' French provincial style house with its dark roof and stonework. It seemed out of place compared to the surrounding ranch style homes. She went through a side gate, and entered the backyard, thankful the celebration wouldn't be inside her mother's spotless house with white carpet and expensive leather furniture.

The five-acre spread hadn't changed much. The fort her brothers made with Dad could use a fresh coat of paint. Several creosote bushes lined the property. For a second, she was a little girl collecting a tarantula in a can. Proudly, she'd shown her catch to Dad. He called her his little biologist. Because of his encouragement, she loved teaching science to her first-grade students.

She smiled recalling the shriek Mother let out when she held her prized tarantula in her hand. *"What is wrong with you? Those things are dangerous."* Her mother then eyed her from head to toe. *"Honestly, Birdie, your dress is filthy."*

"Field work can be messy," Birdie repeated a line Dad had told her and skipped away.

"Something smells good." Kristy turned to her.

"Dad's grilling steaks." The tangy aroma of barbequed meat filled the air. "I'd better go say hi to him." She set the brownies on a table and walked over to her father.

"Glad you made it, shortstop." Dad wiped his hands on his Barbeque King apron. "Hope you're hungry." He embraced her with a bear hug.

"Starved. How long till the food's ready?"

He let go of her and went back to the steaks. "'Bout half an hour."

"Then I'll get myself a drink. See you when the steaks are done." She walked under the covered patio where Granny, Kristy, and Zack were milling around with several others.

Reaching into one of the red plastic bins filled with ice, she snagged a longneck Corona.

"Hey, honey, grab me an orange soda," Granny requested.

Fishing through several cans of diet coke and root beer, she found an orange colored can in the bottom of the blue bin. Her hands were chilled as she handed the can to Granny.

"You're such a dear." Granny squeezed her hand.

Kristy pushed in next to her and bounced on her toes. "Think your mom made her famous potato salad?"

"Probably." Birdie could search for Mother to see if she needed help, but she knew where that would lead. Endless lectures about every one of her perceived faults. She'd pass on that fun experience.

"Mickey's coming, right?" Zack moved behind her. "She makes the best macadamia cookies."

"Josie got me hooked on her snickerdoodles," Kristy chimed in.

"To be honest, everything Mickey bakes is delicious," Granny agreed. "And I plan to sample tons of dessert along with the biggest juiciest steak."

"Aren't you on a special diet?" Kristy asked.

"All the food here is pretty special." Granny shrugged.

Birdie knew that look. Granny would do whatever she darn well-pleased.

"Good to see you." Auntie Mickie enveloped Birdie in a lavender scented embrace.

"Everyone loves your desserts." Being with her aunt reminded her of making chocolate chip cookies in her aunt's kitchen. She let her stir, didn't get upset when a little batter got on the floor, and even let Birdie lick the batter spoon.

"That's why you're my favorite niece." Her aunt let her go.

"What about me?" Mia came up.

"You're pretty darn special, too." Auntie Mickie hugged Mia. "Anyway, I'd better help Al set out the desserts." She skittered off.

"Good to see you, cuz," Mia said. "This reminds me of the old days."

"Except we're not sneaking beers anymore."

"We were pretty creative. The one time we got caught, your dad just let us go."

"He's the best." Birdie uncapped her beer and took a long swig. Nothing like a cold one on a hot afternoon.

"Are you talking about me?" Dusty came up and rubbed Mia's baby bump.

"Of course, cowboy." Mia kissed his cheek.

"I'm gonna get us a table," Granny said.

Birdie glanced toward the house, spotting Mother wearing a cocktail dress and high heels. Only her mother would dress up for a barbeque. Habit had Birdie running her hand over her hair to make sure her spiral locks were in place. "Guess I'd better see if she needs help."

"Glad it's not me." Mia gave her a thumbs-up.

"Way to be supportive, cuz." Birdie finished her beer, tossed the bottle in the trash can, and headed for the table. "Hey, Mother," she gave the obligatory kiss on the cheek. "Can I do anything for you?"

"You're such a doll," her mom gushed, most likely because she had an audience. "Bring out the platter of deviled eggs in the fridge."

"Sure thing."

CHAPTER 14

After carrying countless trays and bowls and refilling the bins with sodas, Birdie headed toward the closest of the four octangular tables covered with yellow checkered tablecloths and striped umbrellas.

Zack had two beers in his hand. "Want one?"

"Definitely."

"You up for horseshoes? We can play against Kristy and Clint."

Clint must've got there when Birdie had been busy. "You okay, Granny?"

"You bet. Myrtle should be here any minute. Enjoy your game."

"In that case, let's show 'em how it's done." She followed him to the sand pit appreciating how great he looked in Wranglers.

"Ready to lose?" she called to Kristy and Clint.

"You wish," Kristy called. "We're gonna smear you."

"Ten dollars says you don't. I'll even let you guys go first." Birdie reached into her jeans and took out her money and handed it to her friend.

"You're on."

Kristy and Clint ended up winning, but she still had fun.

After their game, Dad stood in the center of the yard with a platter of meat. "Steaks are ready."

"Let's get in line." Zack put his hand on the small of her back and headed for the food.

Minutes later, Birdie held her plate and took the empty chair by Granny.

Myrtle sat on Granny's other side. "Good to see you again." The lady wore a hot pink blouse, pink capris, and even pink sunglasses.

"I see you're into pink today." Birdie gave a thumbs-up. "I like it."

"Thanks."

"She loves themes," Kristy chimed in while she sat across the table by Clint. "One day, she wore a black evening dress complete with pearls and pumps. Another, she went Hawaiian and even wore a hula skirt."

"You only live once." Myrtle held up her glass of wine. "And I believe in living life to the fullest."

"To life," Granny toasted.

Zack moved in next to her. His leg brushed hers, and she

could swear something sparked between them. Her feelings were growing for him.

"Did you just shock me?"

Birdie batted her lashes and said, "I would never do that."

"Hey," Garrett set his plate down filled to the brim, kitty-corner to Birdie, and pulled out a chair on the other side for Josie.

Birdie got up and plucked out a strand of her brother's hair. "Birthday boy, is that gray I see?"

"Nope. You've gone loco," Garrett made the crazy sign with his finger.

"See what I have to put up with. He thinks because he's a year older than me he can boss me around." Birdie moved back to her seat.

"Me, bossy?" Garrett folded his arms. "What about you?"

Several people at their table snickered.

"You can be a bit hardheaded." Granny patted her hand. "But that's one of the reasons we all love you."

"Thanks, I think?"

"She's got you pegged." Garrett let out a loud laugh.

"Well, you're just as bad. And quoting Granny, I love you anyway." Birdie gave him a smug look.

"You two are always competing." Kristy waved a hand. "One time it's who's the best at roping. Then it's who can run the fastest or who's smarter or who has the better car. Just about anything gets them into a showdown."

"Try growing up in a house full of brothers. I had to learn to stand up for myself." For most of her life, Birdie longed for a sister. As a consolation she had her cousin and luckily she had lived nearby.

"Now she's playing the sympathy card. How many times has she hogged the bathroom … sometimes for hours?" Henry patted Birdie's shoulder and took an empty chair on the opposite side. "But I forgive you."

"You're such a brat."

"No name calling." Granny held up one hand. "This is a party."

And just like that, everyone was back to eating and laughing.

Josie twisted a long blonde curl around her finger. "I'm thrilled you'll be here for the summer. When are we going to lunch?"

"Count me in." Kristy flipped her long hair behind her shoulders.

"How about a spa day?" Mia rubbed her belly. "I could use some relaxation."

"What do you say, Granny? Would you and Myrtle want to go?"

"Definitely."

Dad stood up at the table next to her and cleared his throat. "It's hard to believe that twenty-seven years ago, this guy was born." He walked over to Garrett and put his hands on his shoulders. "We've had some trying years but look at him now. Married with a baby on the way. To Garrett."

"To Garrett," everyone said.

Zack clinked her glass.

Her heart skittered. Damn, he's gorgeous.

"Now, get over here and blow out some candles." Mother held a cake shaped like a white Stetson, and everyone sang.

Garrett blew out all twenty-seven candles.

"Bravo, son." Dad added. "What'd you wish for?"

"I've already got everything I've ever wanted." Garrett grinned at his wife as he sat down next to her.

Birdie got up to pass out plates. "Great party," she said to her mom.

"It has turned out well. I appreciate your help." Mother sounded civil.

Birdie held her breath waiting for a snarky remark, but it didn't come.

After delivering all the slices of cake, she finally got a chance to sit down and take a bite. "This is heaven."

"Even if it's not chocolate?" Zack asked.

"It's an Auntie Mickie creation. Need I say more?" Kristy chimed in.

"Nope." His eyes caught with Birdie's, and he gave her a sexy grin.

His attention always seemed to drift her way making her feel special. She found herself smiling back.

The man was sin on a stick.

She couldn't wait to be held in his arms as she danced with him again. Hell, who was she kidding? She wouldn't mind kissing him again.

CHAPTER 15

Garrett made quite a haul. T-shirts, gift cards, even a new saddle. Then he held the gift Birdie got him. The coffee mug with *World's Greatest Brother.*

"You told me I'm your favorite," Henry called.

"She said the same to me." Tyler gave her a mock frown.

"My favorite switches depending on the day." That comment should hold them off for now.

Garrett held up an oversized pillow designed with his face. "Kristy, you're nuts."

"Got it just in case you forgot what you look like."

"Just make sure Josie doesn't snuggle up to the wrong version of you," Henry laughed.

"Never, my love." Josie planted a kiss on his mouth.

"Oh, to be young and in love." Granny fanned her face.

A tinge of jealousy at seeing such a happy couple rattled deep in Birdie's heart. Jealousy. Ridiculous.

"Thanks everyone for the presents." Garrett took off his hat and waved it. "Now, let's get the celebration started."

The sun set on the horizon as a Brad Paisley song played from speakers near the sliding glass doors. Garrett led his wife to a grassy area where Auntie Mickie, Uncle Al, and a few other people were dancing.

Zack stood behind Birdie's chair. "Wanna dance?"

"Yes." The moment his warm hand held hers a tingle shivered up her arm. Why was it whenever she was near him, she wanted more contact?

They two-stepped to "Beers and Sunshine."

"Can you believe the lyrics to this song? With beer and sunshine any guy will get lucky."

"I'm feeling lucky tonight," Zack's deep voice crooned. He spun her under his arm, and they were back to two-stepping.

"Does that line work with other women?"

"Don't know. Never tried it." He tugged her a little closer as they danced across the floor. "I'm glad you're here." He twirled her away from him and then back.

"Me, too." This might not be how she had planned to spend her summer, but she liked being with Zack. Not only was she enjoying her time with him, but he was turning out to be an excellent friend.

The song ended and Granny came up to her looking tired.

"Is something wrong?"

"Not at all. Myrtle's driving me home."

"I can do that." She jerked out of Zack's arms frantic that something might happen to her grandmother. "I've gotta go."

"Calm down. I'm just worn out from the day."

"Is there a problem?" Zack asked.

"I think she overdid it at the party. This was her first night out since her surgery." Birdie couldn't help worrying.

"I'm fine. Really."

"Actually, I think I'm more worn out than her," Myrtle said. "I'll make sure she gets home safely."

"Okay but call me if you need me."

"I will." Granny took Birdie's hand. "Enjoy the party. I'll see you at home later." She waved as she reached the gate.

Zack put his arm around her. "Don't stress."

"It's hard sometimes. Granny can be so stubborn." She flashed him a smile.

"That makes her a fighter. Just like someone I know."

"I'm not stubborn."

"I didn't say that. I said you're strong and beautiful."

She hit his arm. "And you're quite the charmer."

"Thanks."

"Make it Shake" played.

"It's time to line dance." Kristy and Clint came up next to her. "Come on, guys."

Mia and Dusty ended up in front of her. Garrett and Josie next to her on the right.

The night went on.

At some point she slow danced to "Good Thing." She

leaned into Zack's chest and breathed him in, reveling in his masculine scent. She could get used to being held in his arms. "This is my new favorite song."

He came in nearer and whispered in her ear, "You are now my new favorite everything."

She found herself snuggling in closer and laying her head against his chest.

At close to eleven, the party came to a halt. Zack walked her out to the car. "Wanna head for the Boot Scoot?"

"Not tonight. I better get home and check on Granny." It had been hours since she left with Myrtle.

"Some other time then."

"Absolutely."

"Hmm …" He slowed his steps. "I have a couple of dirt bikes at home. Do you ride?"

"Of course. Rode a minibike at five." After months of bugging Tyler, he finally caved. "The first time I gave it gas, I dove face first into a creosote bush."

"But you didn't give up."

"It's not in my nature."

"That's what makes you sexy as hell." He put his arm around her shoulder. "Would tomorrow work for riding?"

She got out her phone. "Granny has a doctor's appointment at ten. I should be free later in the afternoon."

"Is two okay?"

"Sure."

They reached her car. Zack put a hand on the side of the

door. His lips pressed against her cheek. "Have a safe drive home."

Was that all? No way would he get away that easy. She put her arms around his neck and brought her mouth to his, giving him a searing kiss. She was breathing hard when she pulled away. "Sweet dreams."

"You too, sunshine." He tipped his hat and walked backwards to his car.

Birdie shook her head. Time with him might be just what she needed for now.

Maybe not. She couldn't risk developing feelings for him.

CHAPTER 16

Zack couldn't help whistling as he parked in front of the farmhouse with two dirt bikes in the back of his uncle's truck. He spotted two people on horses riding up behind him.

"Hey, Zack." Garrett dismounted as did his wife.

His friend was happily married, but Zack missed the wild times they'd had as bachelors. In fact, he'd lost a great wingman for picking up women.

"What's up?"

"Birdie asked me to stop by and see Granny," Garrett said.

"Thanks for letting me borrow your bike."

"It's just collecting dust in your barn. But not for much longer." Garrett's smile brightened. "Another month, and my garage will be done."

"It's great seeing you." Josie insisted on a hug.

"You too," Zack hugged her back. As a fellow time traveler from the past, they had an unusual connection. A bond.

Garrett wrapped his arm around Josie's shoulder.

Birdie must've heard them talking because the front door flung open. "I'm glad you could make it. Granny's doing well, but I'd rather not leave her alone for long."

"That's what family's for." Josie embraced Birdie. "Besides, it gives me a chance to get your grandmother to gossip about the Smith family who lived here in the late 1800's."

"Let me know if you learn anything juicy." This property had a long history of interesting characters.

"I will."

"See you guys later." Garrett and Josie walked into the house.

"You ready." He motioned to his vehicle.

"Hell, yes." She pointed to the bed of the truck. "I get the red Yamaha."

"It's Garrett's bike."

"I haven't seen it before. When did he get it?"

"A few months ago. He bought it off a friend at work."

"I bet he got a good deal."

"Of course." Garrett could haggle anything down. Zack drove onto the highway.

"Where we going?"

"Coyote Hills." It should be fairly empty giving him plenty of alone time with her.

"The last time I went up there, I think I was thirteen.

Garrett and I snuck off at dawn and rode from our house in Oak Hills."

"That must've taken a couple of hours."

"We were gone all day. When we got home, Mother was livid—at me." She rolled her eyes.

"Not at Garrett." In his mind, he could understand if her mom had been worried.

"Of course not. He was a boy expected to do thrill-seeking things."

"And you?"

"Mother had planned to take me shopping, and then lunch at a teahouse." She scrunched up her face. "Imagine me sipping tea and eating finger sandwiches."

"I can see it now. You wearing a frilly dress and holding up your pinkie finger on the handle of your a fancy teacup." The sides of his mouth tipped up.

"You know way too much about this."

"Your niece, Charlotte, loves tea parties, and I'm just the right sucker to play along with her." He recalled how the little girl conned him into sitting in a small chair while she pretended to serve tea and crumpets.

"I'm jealous. She's never asked me to join in."

"If you stick around long enough, I'm sure you'll get an invitation."

"You know I'm leaving in another month."

"Thirty days should be plenty of time." He really wished she would stay longer and wouldn't mind developing this crush of his into something more. While she was here, he'd do his best to woo her. Show her that they could be good together.

Still, deep down he had to remember she had a life in another state. While his life in this century was precarious at best.

Surrounded by Joshua trees and creosote bushes and wide-open desert, there wasn't a single person in sight. He pulled down the tailgate. She immediately grabbed the ramps, set them in place, and unbuckled the straps for the red motorcycle. He set a helmet on her head. By the time he'd freed his own bike, her motorcycle had been wheeled to the ground, and she mounted it. "Slow poke." She revved the engine as he got on his bike. "First one to the fairy chimney wins."

"Where's that?"

"The tall thin spires of rocks." She was off with a good lead.

Giving his bike gas, he shifted gears. The wind whooshed against his helmet as he sped along the open desert terrain. As much as he tried, he couldn't get ahead of her. But he didn't mind. He flew over a hill and let out a whoop.

When she reached the rock formation, both her arms waved in the air as she slowed down. "I won," she shouted.

"You gave yourself a head start." He eased his hand off the throttle.

"Not as much as you did when we raced horses at the riverbed." She removed her helmet and shook out her hair, making him long to run his fingers through the tresses.

"Touché." He had been pretty sneaky that time.

She smiled.

"You said you rode bikes, but I never expected you to be a pro."

"I can do lots of things." With one hand on her hip, her mouth twitched upward.

Damn she's sexy. "Wanna ride over to Curiosity Pond?"

"Sure. Think we'll see any desert tortoises or maybe even a chuckwalla?"

"What's a chuckwalla?" he asked. There were so many things he hadn't learned about this century.

"The scientific name is Sauromalus ater. It's from the iguana family. There used to be hundreds of them living in the High Desert until people plowed down terrain in order to put up housing tracts and strip malls."

"You don't care for progress?"

"Not when it ruins habitats. I'm really into the environment."

"We've got that in common. I hate it when farms and ranches are mowed down and replaced by townhouses." What he wanted to say was he'd rather see more open space like in the nineteenth century. "What color are your chuckies?"

"I like the nickname. They're usually brown so they camouflage well with the desert. If I see one, I'll show you." And she took off.

Once again leaving him in her dusty trail.

CHAPTER 17

Birdie crouched next to Zack on the edge of the pond. "There's one."

Zack squinted and noticed a large lizard with stocky legs and a flat head lounging underneath a bush. "It's kinda ugly."

"But interesting. When I was younger, I used to pick them up. They're really docile." She shook her head. "I learned in college it's best to leave them alone, so they don't catch a virus from us."

"Did you major in science?" He liked school but that ended when he was twelve.

"Liberal arts. I took a smattering of all subjects, but I found myself really enjoying biology and zoology classes."

"You're a bookworm."

"Nothing wrong with being a nerd." She brushed a strand of hair behind her ear.

"Not at all. Especially one as pretty as you." With her green eyes and full mouth, he'd been drawn to her from the very start. But the more time he spent with her, the more he liked her go-for-it attitude.

"Thanks."

"You're welcome."

A jack rabbit hopped along the trail.

She whispered, "Looks like we have company. It's a Lepus californicus gray."

"Now, you're just showing off." Figuring she wouldn't want to hear how he used to cook hares over an open fire, he kept his thoughts to himself. "Ready to eat?"

"I'm starving."

He untied a large canvas bag strapped at the back of his bike. Together they spread out a blanket. "Hope you like roast beef sandwiches." He offered her a baggie.

Her eyes lit up. "That's one of my favorites. Did Garrett tell you?"

"Yep. He also said you like Funyuns and Dr. Pepper." He handed her a bag of chips and a can. Then he took out a container. "I came up with chocolate chip cookies on my own."

"From Auntie Mickie's bakery. You're a saint."

"I do my best."

"It isn't fair. You know all about me, and I don't even know your favorite food." She tilted her head.

"Burger and fries. In-N-Out's the best." This century had plenty of advantages like frozen dinners and fast food. It made him wonder what his family would think of all this century had to offer.

"In-N-Out is on the way to Granny's doctor. Next time I take her in for an appointment, I'll get you a double-double and fries. You like animal style?"

"Heck, yes." His mouth watered thinking about fries topped with special sauce, cheese, and onions.

"My friends in Colorado think it's disgusting."

"Well, this friend in California loves them." He polished off his sandwich. "This comes in a close second to burgers." Reaching in his bag, he took out a cola.

"What do you like to do when you're not working?"

"Ride horses and motorcycles, dance, play pool." That's about as exciting as his life got.

"If I had more free time, I'd like to see the Grand Canyon and take a mule ride to the bottom and even go river rafting."

"That sounds great, especially the mule ride." He wouldn't mind going with her.

"I'm hearing a but …" She folded her hands together. "I'm sure your uncle would give you a week or two off."

"Maybe a few days. The farm is crazy busy."

"You sound like Tyler."

"I'll take that as a compliment. I like all your brothers. They're good guys." Kristy might have saved him, but the Kellogg men were all open and friendly.

"What about your family?"

"My parents are okay." Given it would be impossible for them to visit here, he pushed away his melancholy thoughts.

"We just don't always see eye to eye on what I should be doing. They think farm life is beneath them." At this rate, his nose should have grown about a foot. He wished he could be honest. But Kristy and he came up with this cover story in order to keep his secret safe.

"I know what it's like when you don't live up to a parent's expectation. Luckily, I've got Dad on my side."

She bought into his lie, making him feel like a heel.

He had a wonderful family. A family he missed every day.

"How did you end up moving here?"

"Umm ..." Guilt made it hard to think. He hated deceiving her. Even more, he hated lying about his family. "My aunt and uncle visited us when I was in grade school. Uncle Will and I hit it off. Then my parents had a falling out with them. A few years ago, they found me on Facebook and invited me to come visit whenever I wanted." He took off his hat and wiped away a bead of sweat dripping down his forehead. "Best move I ever made."

"Would you ever consider relocating somewhere else, or is this your forever place?" She quirked a brow.

"Nothing's set in stone." Last year, when Josie disappeared through a time portal to the 1890's, Garrett asked his Uncle Al for advice because he understood astrophysics and the theory of time travel. With his help, they were able to bring Josie back to the future. At the time, Zack had considered going back. But despite missing his family, he decided he liked his life here.

"Don't I know it." She plucked a cookie from the

container, took a bite, and handed it to him. "This is delicious. Try it."

His body stirred anticipating if her sensuous mouth tasted as sweet as the chocolatey temptation.

"Is something wrong?"

"Not a thing." Except for the desire bulging in his jeans.

"Your parents' property has large stalls for horses, but you don't seem to own any."

"Mother hates horses. Unlike her, I've always been a tomboy."

"Not being so girly makes you fun to be around."

"You're sweet." She put her hand on top of his.

"I was hoping for handsome or sexy."

"You already know that you're a hunk." She fanned her face and gave him a saucy smile.

He leaned over and kissed her, reveling in the taste of her.

CHAPTER 18

Perfection. That's how Birdie described her day so far at the spa. What could be better than spending time with a select group of friends and family—namely Mia, Kristy, Granny, Myrtle, and Josie. Finished with their facials, her feet soaked in the swirling, warm water for mani pedis.

Her phone chirped. She picked it up and chuckled because she'd told Zack she'd be getting her nails done today.

"What's so funny?" Mia asked.

"This," she held up a photo of a poodle with purple fingernails.

"That's crazy," Granny giggled.

"I know, right?" She quickly sent him a smiley face emoji and shut her phone.

"Who sent that?" Kristy eyed her sideways.

"Ursula." Birdie lied. Just a little white lie. Zack and she were friends but knowing this group, they'd make a big deal out of nothing. Especially if they learned that she and Zack were texting almost every day.

"Tell her thanks for sharing," Josie said.

"Will do."

"We all set for the beach trip?" Granny asked her friend.

"Sure am."

"What trip?" Mia said as her manicurist painted her toenails light blue.

"Birdie, Carol, and I are going to Sandy Shores the last weekend in August." Myrtle raised a finely arched brow. "Since I'm taking my motorhome, you're more than welcome to come. There's plenty of room, or you ladies could pitch a couple of tents."

"Sounds good to me," Kristy chimed in.

The past trips with Myrtle had been great. Birdie couldn't help grinning. The lady was a master at parking an RV.

"What about the men? Are any of them invited?" Mia asked.

"The more the merrier."

"My mom and I used to take the train to the ocean for the day." Josie gave a faraway look. "I've always wanted to camp on the beach. Sleeping where you can hear the waves pounding would be heavenly."

"So it's settled," Granny said.

"I'm excited." Kristy rubbed her hands together. "It's been forever since the gang went anywhere."

"It'll be my last hurrah before the baby comes." Mia rubbed her rounded belly.

After this trip Birdie would be returning to Colorado. Her summer vacation over.

Done with their pedicures, the women made their way to the manicure tables. Birdie looked down at her sparkly gold toenails. The color matched her happy mood.

"Who's going to the concert tonight?" Mia asked.

Kristy raised her hand. "Clint's taking me."

"Did you tell him you're in love with the lead singer?" Birdie couldn't help teasing.

"It's not exactly love."

"Just a major crush. You should have seen her when they played at the Wagon Wheel. I'm pretty sure she slipped the guy her number." Mia rolled her eyes.

"I did not. Josie will you be there?"

Birdie thought about saying, *Way to deflect,* but figured her friend already had enough razzing.

"Garrett's taking me. I know nothing about the band Rocky Surprise. How should I dress?" Josie's eyes rounded.

"They're a country band so it's casual. A sundress or jeans and a T-shirt would suffice," Mia said. "I'll be the one in a muumuu."

"I think you look adorable" Granny said.

"You kinda have to say that. This is your great-granddaughter."

"Well, it's true."

"Carol and I will be missing this concert in the park. We'll be there in spirit," Myrtle added.

"Hot dates?" Kristy placed her hand under the nail dryer.

Granny blushed. Something she rarely did. Good for her.

"Let's meet near the snack bar at six." Kristy examined her nails and opted for a ying-yang symbol on her pinkie finger.

And just like that, tonight's plans were made.

CHAPTER 19

Three hours later, Birdie heard the rumble of Zack's car signaling his arrival. She glanced in the mirror by the front door, adjusted the straps on her sundress, and snagged a light blue sweater from a hook.

Opening the door, she found Zack about to knock.

"Hey." He handed her a bouquet of mixed flowers.

She held the flowers close to her face to hide the blush burning her cheeks. Zack was a good friend. A friend she was tempted to make as a friend with benefits.

"You look beautiful," he said in a low sensual voice.

Noting how his muscles filled out the black T-shirt he wore, she sucked in a deep breath.

Realizing the flowers were still in her hand, she sniffed the bouquet. "Let me put these in water and I'll be ready.

Carnations are my favorite, and Granny's gonna love the daisies."

"Where is she?"

"Her and Myrtle met friends for dinner." She set the vase on the kitchen table.

"Those two do keep busy."

"Nothing slows them down. Not even a heart attack. I wish I were more like Granny."

"You're perfect just as you are."

That silly, sappy comment made her swoon.

Minutes later, they were on the road heading toward the park. "Have you heard the band Rocky Surprise before?"

"I have. The lead singer reminds me of Luke Bryan. My cousin's crazy about him."

"So I've heard. Wonder if Clint knows about her crush?"

"I'm sure he does."

"I think Kristy and Clint are cute together."

He shrugged.

"You don't like Clint?"

"He's fine."

"But—"

"She tends to lead with her heart. I just don't want to see her get hurt."

"That's sweet. You're her protector."

"She's like a little sister to me." That made him think about his sister, Sophia. Two years younger than him, he and his brother John always kept an eye on her. Made sure nothing bad ever happened. But she had grown up and married. Had her second child before he left. Probably had nieces or nephews he'd never see.

His family had lived their lives. Married. Had children. Died. He hadn't been there to share celebrations, or worse, mourn losses. Sometimes the ache of separation gnawed at him.

He hadn't been there for his family, but … he could be here for Kristy.

"She's lucky to have you around."

"Thanks." He turned off on Park Avenue.

"What's your favorite thing about working at the farm?"

"The horses. They act like big dogs."

"Have you taught any to fetch?"

"Not yet." He said with a chuckle as he imagined Cinnamon fetching his hat.

"I miss having my own horse."

"You don't have one in Colorado."

"Can't afford the board." She let out a long sigh. "Besides, after I had to put Sugar down … well … she was one of a kind."

"I feel the same way about Cinnamon." Although if he were honest, Goldie was the best horse he'd ever owned. Probably because he broke the stallion when he was a teen.

"I wanted to barrel race Sugar. Never got the chance"

"I take it your mom wouldn't allow it."

"Exactly." She fisted her hands. "Enough about me. Tyler says he loaned his newest stallion out for stud to your farm."

"He did. I'm anxious to see the foals. We should end up with some outstanding cutting horses."

"Sounds like you're invested in what happens. Is your uncle a good boss?"

"The best." The man had taken him under his wing. He kept his focus on the road. "I have to ask. Think you'll ever move back?"

"No."

Too bad. He longed for more. Swallowing hard, he shook off disappointment.

They reached the entrance to Surprise Valley Park. With acres of lush hillside, they drove behind the lines of cars. Elevated on a hill, the stage came into view first. He pulled into a dirt lot. A guy motioned where to park.

Handing her a blanket from the trunk, he snagged an ice chest.

"Look, there's Tyler." He waved at his friend.

Tyler walked up to the car with April at his side.

"I see you found a sitter." Birdie gave her sister-in-law a hug.

"I did." April smiled. "I love my kids, but …"

"It's date night." Tyler tugged her closer.

As they continued toward the snack bar, Josie and Garrett were hand in hand. "Hey." Garrett fist bumped Zack.

"Love your dress," Josie said to Birdie.

Zack's eyes couldn't help roaming along her bare neck, one he longed to kiss. He heard chatter behind him. Turning, he watched as Mickie and Al, Clint and Kristy, and Dusty and Mia arrived.

"Usual spot?" Al asked.

"This way." Kristy threaded her arm through Clint's.

Typical of a free summer concert, the spots were filling in quickly. Birdie helped Zack lay out their blanket. To their right, Clint and Kristy did the same thing, with Mia and Dusty to their left, and Mickie and Al behind them.

Zack opened the cooler and held two cans. "Corona?"

"Please." She popped the top and took a long drink. "This is perfect."

"Yes, you are." He couldn't resist adding the corny line.

She got out a Tupperware container from her purse. "Look what Granny and I made yesterday. Try one."

"Okay." He bit into a chocolate covered strawberry. Sweetness swirled through his taste buds. "Holy shit, these are good."

"I know, right." He watched her sample one as red juice dripped on her lips. She swept her tongue along the top of her mouth. "Want another one?"

"I'd rather taste you." Talk about a delightful temptation. He kissed her quickly. Longing to deepen their connection, but this wasn't the place.

"Send the strawberries our way." Kristy gave them a thumbs up.

She waved back at her friend. Her cheeks blushing which he found cute.

"Sure thing, cuz." Without taking his eyes from hers, Zack gave the container to Kristy.

"Seeing as you gave away my snack, I hope you packed something good." She leaned over and peeked into the plastic chest. "Fried chicken and Funyons. Interesting combo."

"One of your favorites with a second choice of mine." He got out paper plates and offered her the bucket of chicken. "I'm full of surprises."

"That you are." She snagged a leg. Did she intentionally run her tongue along her top lip to tease him?

"Anyone want dessert?" Mickie brought over a bakery box. "I made brownies plus chocolate chip and pumpkin spice cookies."

"Brownies," Birdie said at the same time as he said, "Chocolate chip." He whispered in her ear, "We can share."

"All right."

He watched as she nibbled on a brownie. "You've got something right there."

"I do?"

He leaned closer and licked the chocolate off with the tip of his tongue. Pulling back, he said, "Got it."

She eyed him while her lips quirked up making her irresistible.

He couldn't help stealing another kiss, getting lost in the swirl of her tongue tangling with his and for a second tuned out the fact they were surrounded by friends and family.

"Welcome, Surprise Valley," a voice boomed from the stage.

The music started with "Let's Kick It," a fast and upbeat original.

"I love this song." Kristy stood up and started dancing.

"You love the lead singer," Mickie bantered as she got up.

"And you love the band," Uncle Al called. "How many times have I caught you at the back of the bakery with a wooden spoon belting out a song?"

"Music helps me create."

"Good one, Auntie Mickie. Admit it you're in love with the drummer." Mia remained lying on the blanket while resting her head in Dusty's lap.

"Guilty." Mickie gave a beaming smile.

"What about me?" Al folded his arms.

Mickie kissed him on the cheek. "I'll keep you for now."

Someday, Zack would like to have a relationship like theirs.

The band switched it up to the line dance "Love You Always." Birdie moved in closer to Kristy, the two of them singing their hearts out.

Zack stayed rooted in his spot enjoying how Birdie smiled as she swayed her hips to the music.

The band took a break and Birdie sat on the blanket next to him. "Miss me?"

"Always."

She batted her eyes and kissed his cheek.

"You're incredibly sexy." He wrapped his arms around her shoulders. As songs played, he rubbed her back, and ran his fingers along her spine before he nonchalantly rested his hand on her thigh. By the time the last song played he was wound up tight.

"We're gonna leave early." Dusty stood with his hand on Mia's back and strolled off.

The band played one more song before the singer announced, "That'll be all folks. Thanks for coming out tonight."

Kristy got out her phone and shook her head. "Eleven already."

Zack and Birdie picked up papers and cans and brought them to the trash as did the others. Blankets were folded. Ice chests grabbed. Everyone packed up.

"Nice seeing you, Birdie." Uncle Al gave her a hug.

Mickie joined in. Then they left.

Kristy came up behind her. "Clint's taking me to his place,"

"Shit. I was hoping we'd head for the Boot Scoot. I'm not ready to go home yet."

"Neither am I." Zack couldn't help smiling as an idea popped in his head. One even better than going to the bar. "There's supposed to be a meteor shower at midnight."

"Sounds good."

"Then let's head for Winchester Hill." He held her hand as they walked to the car.

CHAPTER 20

The sky was chock full of stars as Zack got out of his car on the hillside with a view of the whole valley and opened the door for Birdie.

"Tonight's been pretty tight."

"That's good, right?" After three years in this century, he still didn't get some of the slang.

"Better than good." Water lapped along the bank from the river below. She snagged beers from the ice chest in the back seat and sat on the hood of his Mustang. "Here." She handed him a can.

He moved next to her. "You trying to get me roostered?"

"Roostered?" She laughed, her head back and hair flying in the wind. "Sometimes you say the weirdest things."

"It's an old cowboy expression that means buzzed."

"The word's got a ring to it."

They leaned back on the car, her shoulders pushed against his and a zing shot through his system. He gazed at the star-lit sky.

"Can you pick out the Big Dipper?" Birdie asked.

"Yeah, it looks like a cup." His cousin had shown him the grouping one night while they were sitting on the porch.

"Correct." Her eyes glittered in the moonlight. "What other constellations can you name?"

"The North Star." He'd use the brightest star to keep his bearings when he rode at night.

"That's Polaris. It's in Ursa Minor which is a part of the Little Dipper. Because of the moonlight, most stars are too faint to see without binoculars. Too bad I left mine in Colorado or I could show you." Her tone came out wistful.

"Another time then." He wouldn't mind visiting where she lived. He narrowed his gaze, studying her delicate features. Chucking his thumb under her chin, he gazed into her eyes. "You sure know a lot about stars."

"Astronomy has always fascinated me. Take Orion's belt for example. It's the three dots north of the Big Dipper."

He squinted. "I see it." He didn't get the connection to a belt but figured she'd tell him.

"Anyway, according to the ancient Greeks, he's considered a hunter who chases after a hare with his two hunting dogs in the Lepus constellation." She pursed her lips. "The Sumerians have an even better story. Supposedly, the giant, Orion told the Goddess Artemis he could defeat all Earthly beasts. She sent him a scorpion. The sting killed the giant. In his honor, he has his own constellation with a scorpion's stinger always nearby."

"Those people had a great imagination."

"Nothing wrong with getting lost in fantasy every now and then." She bumped his shoulder. "It's no different than watching an action movie or getting lost in a good romance novel."

"To be honest, I never read romance." He took her hand.

"You're such a guy."

"Thank you." He threaded his fingers through hers. "You're cute." He leaned over to kiss her, but she pushed him away.

"I hate cute. Call me smart. Even a tomboy. But never cute."

"How 'bout hot? Would that be up to your standards?"

"I like the way you think."

Splaying his fingers through the thickness of her hair, she smiled at him. Desire hummed through his body.

"Look. A shooting star!" She pointed to the east. "Make a wish."

"I've already got my wish. I'm with you." With her arms around his neck, she fit perfectly like she were made for him. Her breath warmed his cheek.

He peppered kisses down her long throat and caressed the hollow of her collarbone. His hands rubbed slow circles on her back, spiking his body's heat. The need to taste her had his heart beating hard and fast as he brushed his mouth against the softest, sweetest lips.

"Do you have to smell so damn good?" her voice became low and sultry.

"You're the one who smells like wildflowers." The scent drove him to distraction.

She flicked her tongue along his top lip and when she added a little bite, he claimed her mouth. Sparks swept over every square inch of him. They tangled their tongues in a tantalizing dance. Heat skyrocketed and wound its way through every cell in his body. His mind blurred into the sort of bliss only an epic kiss can deliver. An unraveling kind of kiss that had his whole body full of passion and fever and heat.

They leaned back on the hood of the car. Her hands inched up his shirt, her body pressed against him. The kiss grew hotter and more intense. He kissed her like a man hungry for her every breath, cupping her butt in his palms and towing her nearer.

Her fingers roamed along his chest, driving him wild with every touch. Her kisses ghosted against his neck, and she gave a little nip on his chin.

This woman was gonna kill him. His fingers skimmed along her legs bunching her dress at her waist and gliding to the lace of her panties. She quivered as he ran a fingertip along the edge. He cupped the material, his other slid to her stomach and then her breast.

Every instinct he had was to make love to this woman in his arms and make sure she remembered the passion that raged between them. Only her silk panties separated his hand from her hot bare flesh. She let out a whimper.

"You like that?"

"Yes." She arched up and kissed him.

Choo. Choo. A train sounded in the distance.

She jerked and bolted up. "What time is it?"

He nabbed his phone out of his pocket. "One-fifty."

"I need to go. Granny's got an early doctor's appointment."

"Sure thing." He couldn't resist taking her into his arms and kissing her once more. Then he brought her back to the farmhouse.

Once he got home, he texted her.

Zack: *Thanks for sharing the night with me.*

He added a video of a falling star.

Birdie: *It was spectacular.*

Zack: *Just like you. Sweet dreams.*

CHAPTER 21

Two weeks later, Birdie strolled down to the shore and enjoyed the serenity of the morning. A seagull cawed as she watched the waves roll in and out. A sailboat glided across the horizon. She'd been on whale watching excursions and even a trip to Catalina, but sailing seemed like it'd be more intimate and personal. One of these days, she'd add that to her list of adventures.

Late yesterday afternoon, she and the women arrived at Sandy Shores Campground. Myrtle and Granny came in an RV, while she, Mia, and Josie rode in Kristy's car. She couldn't help smiling, recalling how they all sang at the top of their lungs with the songs on the radio. Yep, this was already turning out to be a wonderful trip.

And it would become even more entertaining when Zack, Dusty, and Garrett joined them.

Her phone chimed with a text.

Zack: Please tell me we'll see one of these.

He sent her a Tiktok clip with a manatee swimming in the ocean while "You've Got a Friend in Me" played.

She couldn't help laughing as she searched the net for information.

Birdie: *Wrong ocean. If we lived in Florida, our chances of seeing a Trichechus would be better.*

Zack: *It was worth a try.*

Birdie: *We have a good chance of seeing a Eubalaena or maybe a pod of Delphinus delphis.*

Zack: *Seeing a whale or dolphin would be awesome.*

A photo of a dolphin jumping in the air showed on her screen.

Zack: *Better go feed the horses. Can't wait to see you later.* He added a smiley face.

Who would have thought texting about sea creatures could be so entertaining.

"Hey, girl." Kristy came up holding two steaming mugs.

"You read my mind." She took the cup and motioned for her friend to sit on the towel next to her. "Is anyone else up?"

"Granny and Myrtle. They're making breakfast."

"I hope it's blueberry pancakes."

"Of course. Along with scrambled eggs and bacon." Kristy sipped her coffee. "When we get old, I hope we're just like those two."

"Only if I get to drive the motorhome."

"You've got it." Kristy tapped her cup with Birdie. "To friends."

Dawn lit the sand with an orangish yellow glow. "It's pretty here."

"And quiet. When the guys arrive, things will change."

"I know. I can hear Zack and Garrett whooping it up when they run into the water." Kristy hunched her shoulders and wrapped her arms around her knees. "I wish Clint could have made it."

"Next time."

"This beach trip should be a yearly thing. That'll give you a good excuse to come back."

"We'll see." Next year, she hoped to stay in Colorado for the summer. Still, she did enjoy hanging with her friends and Granny. After Granny's heart surgery, she'd need to spend some time with her. Maybe a week or two.

"You could bring Ursula. I like your roommate."

"So do I." Ursula was her best friend in Colorado. Kristy her best friend since grade school. "Right now, I just wanna enjoy today."

"How are things going with you and Zack?"

"We're friends."

Kristy tapped her arm. "I saw you two at the concert. Friends don't look at each other like you two do."

"I'm leaving in three days. Zack knows that."

"Do you want more?" Kristy arched a brow.

"Even if I did, long distance relationships never work."

"Just promise me you won't break his heart. I'll end up picking up the pieces."

"You're making this a big deal. Zack's just a friend. Nothing more. Period." *Even if I do like kissing him.*

Stick with the plan, she told her heart.

CHAPTER 22

Around four p.m., wet, soggy, and somewhat sunburned, Birdie, Kristy and Josie held their boogie boards. They walked toward Mia splashing at the shoreline. Given her condition, she had opted for staying safe. Her cousin reminded Birdie of an egg with legs and a face.

"It was fantastical." Josie's voice reminded Birdie of a Disney princess on overdrive.

"Don't you mean fantastic?" Kristy squinted.

Josie placed one hand on her hip. "Fantastical means strange and wonderful. Riding those waves was a combination of the two."

"Good point." Okay, her brother's wife used interesting vocabulary. Nothing wrong with being a little different. Birdie nabbed her towel, dried off, and sat in her yellow and white beach chair.

"How's the water?" Granny asked as she lounged under a big umbrella.

"Perfect. Just like this day."

"Ain't that the truth," Kristy chimed in. "What time are the guys getting here?"

Mia checked her phone. "They left two hours ago so they should be here soon. Think we should head back to the RV and put together something for dinner?"

"No need. We're having hot dogs and potato salad," Myrtle said, taking a sip from her can of Pina Colada.

Granny clicked her margarita can with her friend.

"You two know how to party." Kristy laughed. "I like it."

"This is nothing." Granny took a sip. "You should have seen me and Gramps in our younger days. We used to sneak beer from his dad and go up in the hayloft to drink."

"And a whole lot more, I'm sure." Myrtle shook her head.

"He was such a character. I miss the old coot every day."

"So do I." Gramps had this no-nonsense way of explaining things to Birdie.

"He used to sit me on his lap showing me an old photo of downtown Hesperia, and we'd pretend we were walking down Main Street in the 1800's." Mia looked up toward the sky.

"Gramps sure could tell stories." Birdie's grandfather had the best sense of humor.

"I think most of his tales were made up." Granny smiled.

Three figures waved from a slight distance.

"The men are here." Josie ran towards Garrett and

jumped into his arms. Mia waddled to Dusty and embraced him.

Kristy took off her sunglasses and twirled them. "You'd think they hadn't seen each other in weeks not a little more than a day."

"Oh, to be young and in love." Granny gave a dreamy look.

Birdie's eyes zeroed in on Zack. He'd stripped off his shirt and even from a few yards away, she could swear he flexed his pecs just for her. Seriously, the guy should be on the cover of Muscle Magazine.

"Zack's quite a man," Granny said with a smirk.

"Yep." Birdie had been caught gawking. Well, how could she not.

A minute or two later, Zack set his towel next to her chair. "Hi." His gaze skimmed her body for a nanosecond, but he quickly focused on her face.

"How was your drive?"

"Not bad until we hit Pacific Coast Highway. But we made it." He stretched his arms above his head. "I see you've been swimming. How's the water?"

"Great. Kristy, Josie, and I were boogie boarding." She held up her board.

"Is it hard?"

"Not really. This was Josie's first time, and she did great."

"Mind giving me some pointers."

"There's not much to it. You swim out a ways, wait for the right wave, and hold onto the board."

"Go ahead and use mine. I'm gonna work on my tan." Kristy motioned to the board next to her.

"Pink. Really?" Zack's mouth quirked up at the sides.

"What's wrong with it?" Kristy lifted her sunglasses.

"Not a thing. Ready?" He offered Birdie his hand to help her up.

She snagged her yellow board. They made their way to the water's edge. "Before we get in, you need to attach your leash to your wrist." They held their boards and dipped under several waves until they reached just past the breakers. "It's good here. Watch me." She took off in the next wave, the force reminded her of soaring. Nothing was better than being outside like this. She couldn't resist making a bottom turn to get into the curl of the wave and doing a 360. Too soon she reached the shore and turned back.

Zack faced the water, paddled into a fairly big crest, and zoomed towards her wearing a wide grin.

Broad shoulders showcased his bulging biceps and triceps. What would it feel like to touch his sexy wet body with her fingertips? Her breath was shallow, panting.

She made it over several waves and caught up to Zack.

"This is awesome." He turned around.

"Told you it was easy." They paddled out further.

Soon, they had company. Josie showed Dusty how to boogie board.

Once the group headed for their campsite, the sun had lowered.

"Wanna help me put up my tent?" Zack asked.

"Sure."

"Garrett loaned me a puptent." He took the bag out of the trunk.

They spread out the parts on the sand. "Are there directions?"

"I don't see any." To be honest, he didn't have a clue what to do.

"Let's start with the tarp." She laid it out on the sand. "You want the windows facing the ocean?"

"Yes. What's next?"

"The poles."

He helped her connect the poles by numbers. Then they weaved the end into an eyelet at each corner.

"This doesn't look right." He tried to raise the tent and it flopped down.

They took everything apart and redid it.

This time it worked.

He pointed to the camper. "Next time, I'm borrowing one of those."

CHAPTER 23

That evening, the gang sat around the campsite toasting marshmallows and drinking beer or canned cocktails.

"Wanna take a walk?" Zack asked. The image of Birdie in a bikini remained etched in his brain. She was beautiful. Tonight, she'd changed into a strapless sundress. More than ready to trail kisses along her neck and taste the salty sea from her body, his mouth watered.

"Sure." She tucked a couple of Corona's from the cooler inside her straw beach bag.

He set a beach towel over his shoulder and offered his hand. Barefoot the soft sand slipped through his toes. They held hands and strolled near the shore as waves crashed against the rocks, misting the air with a briny scent. Moonlight illuminated Birdie's face.

"You're quiet. What's up?"

"Nothing."

She nudged him in the ribs. "Really?

He stopped and gazed into her eyes. "Now that I've got you alone, I've been dying to do this?" His hand tightened around her waist, tugging her into his arms. His mouth dipped down over hers. Heat charged through his body the instant their lips touched.

He nipped at her lower lip, wringing out a "Mmmm" from her that drove him to risk going to the next step teasing, coaxing her mouth open. He ran his tongue along her soft lips and claimed her mouth, dueling and dancing with her tongue.

Water rushed against his ankles, and he stepped back.

"The wave got us," Birdie's tone came a bit squeaky. "I've got an idea. Wait right there." She snagged his towel and jogged up the slight embankment, setting their things down several yards from the water.

Her short dress swished accentuating those gorgeous legs of hers. Legs he liked to feel wrapped around his body. His cock came to attention. Waves rolled over his ankles as if trying to cool his wayward thoughts.

He glanced around the area to see if anyone else shared their beach. For the moment, it belonged to only the two of them.

She ran past him and scooped up a handful of water and threw it at him.

"You little sneak." He sprinted after her and hauled her

into his arms and brought his mouth to the shell of her ear and nipped it. "You're gonna pay for that."

"I was just cooling you off." She ducked out of his hold and darted to the shore where the tide receded. Her hands dug into wet sand.

"What are you doing?" A little water he could handle but he preferred to avoid having sand down his pants.

"Trust me and open your hand?"

He squinted at her.

"Don't be a chicken."

Chicken? His brothers used that taunt to get him to jump into cold river water. He nearly froze his balls off, but after that he'd earned some respect. "Fine."

She released a clump of sand, and something squirmed in his hand.

"What the heck?" He dropped the thing, and it sunk back into the sand and a wave covered it.

"It's a sand crab. They're harmless." The full moon illuminated her face and mischievous smile.

"If you say so." He'd much rather kiss her.

"You should try and get your own."

"I'm game. What do I do?"

"As the tide recedes, look for little V's that are actually air bubbles, dig fast."

Her enthusiasm had him shoving both hands in the sand and scooping up a big mound. He could feel something wiggling in his palms. "It tickles."

"Brush off the sand and you'll be able to see the little guy."

"There's two of 'em. I can't believe it."

"Beginner's luck." She let her crab go.

"Okay, Miss Skeptic, next time I'll get three."

"As if."

Another wave broke. He followed the bubbles and dug. He didn't feel anything wiggling in either hand. He sifted away the sand and laughed. "I didn't catch a one. You jinxed me."

"Well, I got three."

He shifted closer, peaked at her hands, and couldn't help grinning. "Of course, you did. You do love to win."

"It comes from growing up with three brothers."

"I like that you're competitive. It makes you interesting."

"That's the sweetest thing anyone ever said to me." She kissed his cheek.

"You can do better than a measly peck," he couldn't help saying.

"Is that so?" she whispered in his ear and brought her tongue along his neck. Her fingertips traced circles along his forearms and continued up to stroke his biceps. She pressed her lower body against his bulge and rocked her hips.

"You're killing me, sunshine." He wound his arms around her back, towing her in and showing her just how much he wanted her.

"That's the point." Her hands roamed underneath his shirt spiking heat wherever she touched.

His fingers followed the length of her spine and tangled in her hair. He continued devouring her with long dizzying kisses that sent fervor firing through his body. "You taste like sin and heaven." He cupped her face in his hands and gazed into her eyes.

"Isn't that a contradiction?"

"Maybe so, but it describes you. A little bit sweet and a whole lot of sexy." He pushed one strap off her shoulder and feathered kisses along her bare skin.

She panted.

Using his thumb, he traced the outline of her lips. His mouth was on hers again. The feeling like he was on the edge of a dream with the woman he'd been longing to hold for so long. Sparks of desire flashed between them. When they finally pulled away, he was breathing hard.

"Let's find somewhere a little more private," her sultry voice drove him wild.

"Fine with me. You know a place?"

"Around the bend there's a secluded spot below the cliff." She led him to their things picking up her straw bag while he shook out his towel and tossed it over his shoulder. She took his hand. Her softness a stark contradiction to his calloused fingers.

CHAPTER 24

Determined to miss any potential tides sweeping in, they moved along the empty beach, past a huge rock in the water, and up toward the hills away from the beach.

"It's so quiet now. Peaceful." She squeezed his hand. "To think hours ago kids were building sandcastles and people were body surfing or sunbathing."

"Now it's just the two of us." He snagged her around her waist.

"Not exactly. There's plenty of folks at the campground."

"But they're not here now." He leaned down and pressed a kiss to her cheek.

"Obviously." She laughed as they continued back further where the beach curved along the hillside to a sandy area.

The only sounds he heard were the waves lapping against the beach, and his heart thudding hard in his chest.

"Let's sit here." She snagged the oversized towel from his shoulder and spread it out in the sand, sat down, and rifled through her straw bag. "You gonna join me?"

"Yes, ma'am." Trying not to stare at her crisscrossed legs, his voice came out like a croak as he dropped down next to her.

"Beer?"

"You bet."

"To a fantastic day." She clicked her can with his.

"And an intriguing woman." He swigged a big gulp and set his beer in the sand.

She flipped her hair behind her shoulders. "You said this was your first trip to the beach. What do you think?"

"The place is excellent."

"What's your favorite part?"

"Hmm … To be honest, anything that combines water and you in a bikini will always be a win-win for me." He took her beer out of her hand and placed her can in the sand.

Her sassy smile encouraged him.

"If you haven't guessed yet, I like spending time with you," he whispered in her ear and secured his arm around her back, trailing kisses along her throat, and up to her ear.

"Umm," she whimpered, driving him crazy. He angled his mouth over hers, brushing against her lips, tonguing the corner of her mouth while losing his fingers into her soft hair.

She nibbled at his neck, his chin, his mouth. Her nails dug into his shoulders creating a sharp bite that served to churn the fierce hunger feeding his desire. Her hands wandered over his bare skin. She traced her fingernails along his spine creating a shock of tantalizing need.

He stripped his shirt over his head and tossed it aside. Desperate to feel more of her skin, he unzipped the back of her dress and lowered the spaghetti straps off her shoulders, the garment pooled around her hips. He gently nudged her onto her back, all the while teasing and tempting her mouth before reclaiming her lips in another scorching kiss, their tongues melding, and their kisses igniting sparks.

With his eyes glued to hers, he unclasped her bra. "So beautiful."

His fingers roamed along those sweet, sweet curves. He feathered kisses across her neck and meandered down to her breasts. His mouth feasted on a tight bud, laving her nipple with his tongue, teasing the tip and making her wriggle against him.

She arched her back allowing him to circle the center of her nipple.

He kept touching her, scraping his mouth along her abdomen, continuing southward until he kissed the inside of her thigh. "I have to taste you." He waited for her response.

She nodded.

He peeled off her thong, pressing his lips against her waist, exploring every inch of her, encircling his tongue in her belly button, and moving lower. He eased her thighs farther apart and settled her legs over his shoulders, delighting in the scent of her and sucking on her womanly folds, licking her, tasting her and making her buck against his mouth.

"Please, Zack."

His tongue spread light butterfly flicks that made her writhe.

Her fingers combed restlessly through his hair. Begging for release, her hips rotated in rhythmic circles.

He teased with the tip of his tongue, savoring her. Bringing her to the brink of satisfaction and backing away.

She gripped his hair. "More," she pleaded.

"Patience." Feeling her tremble, he continued tormenting and tasting her again and again as she bucked and let out a low gasp. Flicking his tongue along her clit, he brought his thumb against her nub.

She cried out his name as she came.

Turned on beyond belief, he watched as wave after wave seemed to course through her body. He was breathing hard as he lay down next to her.

He gazed into her eyes dark with passion.

"I need you inside me."

A lazy sated smile pulled at his lips as she ran her fingers over the length of him. His bulge grew in response, causing his muscles to coil tightly.

She undid his button and carefully moved down the zipper. As the material parted his cock sprung free. Wrapping her hands around him, she gave it a little squeeze making him even harder. "Yum."

"Later." As much as he'd love to have her mouth on him,

right now he needed to bury his cock inside her pussy. He slipped in a finger, finding her wet and ready. "I want you."

"Hurry."

He moved away, took a condom out of his pocket, shucked his shorts, rolled on the protection, and rose over her. His erection pressed against her entrance. Moonlight glimmered off her eyes. "You sure?"

"Yes."

And in one thrust he filled her tight core. He waited for her to adjust to his size. Reveling in how good this felt. Then he started moving, in and out, his eyes fixed on hers. He slowed his pace causing her to tremble.

"I need ... more." Her head tossed from side to side.

Driven by raw animal need, their bodies rocked together. He possessed her thoroughly raking out her need. Alternating his thrust between slow and quick.

"Faster," she begged.

He picked up speed, staying in tune with her body as they danced the oldest dance in the world. His hands touching and kneading one breast as he brushed kisses to those luscious lips and made love to this responsive woman. He sensed she was about to come and pulled out completely.

"Please. I'm so close."

"Waiting makes it better." He moved his hands under her butt and thrust deeper inside her.

Sweat trickled down his neck as he brought her close to the edge. He took her again and again, driven on by every moan and sigh she made. Her thighs began to quiver, as she pulsed around him and shattered. "Oh, Zack," she cried as she spasmed against his cock.

He plunged into her one last time, and the world exploded around him as he let out a primal roar of completion.

"Fuck," he muttered. It wasn't just that they were compatible in bed, which they obviously were, they seemed compatible in interests.

He could fall for this woman.

ZACK'S FINGERS interwove with hers as they walked back to camp. Warm. Strong. Masculine hands. The simple touch had her core zinging.

"Stay with me tonight?" he asked from outside his pup tent.

"It's pretty small." Her face flooded with heat as she thought about how his thick length had been buried inside her. Nothing small about his cock. She let out a little snort that led to a fit of laughter.

"What's so funny?"

"Nothing. It's just … just …." She sucked in a deep breath. "Small doesn't describe you. Not even a little bit.

"Good to know." He tugged her into his arms and his mouth swooped down and captured hers, kissing her softly, meandering in exploration. He stroked his tongue in a lazy arc over her lips and sent a jolt of desire all the way to her toes.

Closing her eyes, she found herself melting into his body. When he stopped, the loss of contact had her heart palpitating in a rhythm of longing and she inhaled raggedly. Damn, this guy could kiss.

He gazed at her with such tenderness. “Come on. It’ll be cozy.”

Sleep with him again. “Hell, to the yes.”

With a quick zip, the front opened, and she found herself tumbling inside the tent on top of him. His bulge stirred underneath her. “I could get used to this.” His tone was casual as he pressed soft kisses over her eyelids.

Unable to resist exploring his neck, she gave a little nip. Then she soothed the bite with her tongue.

“Ummm,” he rasped into her ear. He seized her mouth with a searing kiss. His lips were commanding and warm and firm.

She exhaled and dug her fingers into his thick hair. His hands roved up and down her back. His touch like a storm brewing full of an electrical charge. Their kisses grew hotter and more intense. She had no idea why air breezed along her thighs or how she ended naked and making love with this incredible man and falling under his spell.

CHAPTER 25

The light of dawn filtered inside the tent. She slept on her side with Zack's arm draped over her. Not wanting to wake him, she carefully peeled his arm off and felt around for her clothing until she found a lump of things near her side. Barely able to sit, she pulled the dress over her head and inched out of the tent.

Zack didn't stir. Last night had been an impulse. A part of her wouldn't mind waking him up for one more quickie, but he seemed so peaceful.

She counted fifteen steps to reach the pop-up tent she shared with Kristy. Darn zipper sounded way too loud. Stepping inside, the zipper was even louder as she closed the opening. She felt her way to the sleeping bag on the right and eased down on top of it with her head cushioned by a pillow.

"How was your night?" Kristy's voice startled Birdie.

"Fine."

"Seeing as you're just getting in, I'm thinking it was better than fine," Kristy said softly.

"We started with a moonlight stroll and, well, I slept with him."

"And that's a problem?"

"Not really." She had three days in town.

"But you'd like more with him."

Hell, yes. Another month would be great. Not that she'd ever admit that out loud.

But she'd be leaving soon. "My home is in Colorado. His is in Surprise Valley. And like I said, Zack and I are having fun. Period." Once she got home, things would go back to normal. Zack would just be a fond memory.

LATER THAT MORNING, the group went to Sandy Shores Island minus Kristy who had to work.

A few hours ago, Zack had been making love with Birdie. It bugged him that she slipped away without saying goodbye. Still, her sassy attitude hadn't changed this morning, so he assumed things were cool.

Zack watched her sign her jet ski rental agreement while humming some upbeat song. "We get three hours, right?"

"That's correct." The clerk nodded.

Birdie put on a life vest covering up that bare stomach

where his hands and mouth had explored. He fought off a groan and stepped up to the counter to sign his own rental agreement.

Holding the key in his hand, he walked out. Jet skis lined the shore. Several feet away Granny and Myrtle were doing donuts. Leave it to these older ladies to start the fun. Dusty sped up and joined the women. Garrett revved his engine and took off with Josie clinging to his waist.

Birdie hopped on her jet ski. He couldn't keep his eyes off her legs hugging the seat. Those same legs had been wrapped around him as she cried out his name.

Not a good time to sport wood. Not in front of everyone. Better focus on the sky or ground beneath his feet.

"You all right?" Mia tapped him on the shoulder. Due in another month, her knit dress showed her large baby bump.

"Just dandy." He'd been caught gawking—at Birdie.

"You like her."

"We're just hanging out." He'd thought about saying they were just friends, but after last night that would be an outright lie.

He had no idea why Mia tilted her head and her lips twitched down.

"What?"

"Wish I could join you." Mia folded her hands on top of her stomach.

"Next time." Zack buckled his last strap on his vest more than ready to catch up to the others. Seconds later he turned on the ignition, twisted the throttle, and jerked forward.

"I saw that." Birdie circled in front of him. "You need some pointers?"

"Not at the moment," he smoothed out his ride and sped up. Driving a jet ski was pretty much like driving a motorcycle. He followed her across the waterway toward the island in the middle of the inlet and admired her skill. Yep. He had it bad.

"This is a good spot to do 360's." She sped around and around.

If she could do it, why couldn't he? After about ten circles, he got dizzy, took his hand off the throttle, and watched Birdie. He liked a woman that didn't get frazzled at the least little thing. No drama with her. She was all about enjoying the moment.

She looped around and slowed next to him. "You give up."

"Nope. Just enjoying the view."

She put her hand above her eyes. "Garret and Josie are coming this way."

His friend moved next to Birdie with Josie on the back of their double Seadoo.

"What's up, bro?" Birdie asked.

"Myrtle wants everyone to race. Mia said she'll judge. You guys in?" Garrett tilted his head.

"Sure," Birdie said without hesitation.

"Me, too." Zack might be a newbie here but that wouldn't stop him from winning.

Back near the shore, the group lined up.

"What are the ground rules?" Granny asked.

"See the three buoys bobbing several yards from the island," Mia said. "You have to circle one of the buoys and come back. The finish line will be the flag right by me."

"Sounds easy enough." Not much different from racing motorcycles to the stone cottage and back. Zack figured he had this.

"Let's make this race interesting, Winner gets bragging rights. Last place person buys everyone lunch," Myrtle said matter of factly.

"How I do like bragging," Granny smirked. "I plan to smoke you kids."

Josie tightened her arms around her husband's waist. Next time, he and Birdie were sharing.

"On your mark. Get set. Go!" Mia shouted.

Zack took off with everyone else. Six engines roared as they raced. Dusty was in the lead, followed by Granny and Myrtle. Somehow, he'd managed to get ahead of Garrett with Josie, and Birdie. But not by much.

On the other side of the inlet, a speedboat went by, leaving a substantial wake heading his way.

Birdie soared over the wave, and yelled, "Yes," as she sailed in the air and landed with ease.

"Hold on tight," Garrett shouted to Josie. His Seadoo was a little larger and seemed to hit the water hard.

Zack attempted to jump the wake, and in an instant found himself tumbling as if in slow motion into seawater. Gasping for air, he made it to the surface. He swam for what seemed like several minutes to his vehicle and put his hand on the end of his seat.

Birdie circled back and slowed. "You okay."

"Just a little wet." He managed to get onto his jet ski.

They rode side by side back to the finish line.

"Sorry you didn't get to race the whole way, sunshine." He told her, feeling a bit guilty because his fall stopped her momentum.

"Sometimes winning is not that important," she said.

The comment made him like her even more.

"Since when, sis?" Garrett called out.

She gave her brother the finger. "We still have another hour on these things, and I plan to enjoy my time." She took off in the direction of the bay.

He didn't hesitate following her. The woman had bravado. She sped up and jumped a wake with ease.

He kept his body tight as he followed suit, this time with ease. The sun shone hot on his arms and chest while spray cooled his face. And he loved every minute of it.

Later, he planned to breathe in her wildflower scent and feather kisses along her neck and down to her collarbone. His cock pressed against his swim trunks. He loved having sex with her, but that wasn't the issue. He was falling for her. Were the feelings returned?

Better concentrate on driving the jet ski and think about shoveling manure with pesky horseflies biting his arms.

~

After a filling dinner at the Crab Shack, Birdie and the rest of the gang got back to camp before nightfall. They'd played several rounds of "Never Have I Ever," near the shore, and everyone went their separate ways. The last rays of pinkish orange vanished from the sky as she stood next to Zack.

All day, his sideways glances and the nonchalant brushes of his hand against her skin had her conjuring up wicked ideas. "Wanna go skinny dipping?"

"Not here."

"Why not?"

"Blame it on watching *Jaws* last week. I'm freaked about being in the ocean when it's dark."

"You're afraid of a little old shark?" she teased.

"Have you seen how many rows of teeth they have?"

"I saw the mechanical Chondrichthyes at Universal Studios."

"I take it that's the scientific name for the fish?" He quirked a brow.

"You know I'm a nerd."

"Which makes you hot." He lugged her into his arms. "I bet you screamed."

"The thing was at least four times my then six-year-old body." She felt herself shiver at the image. "To be honest, I had nightmares for months."

"Looks like I'm not the only one with a shark phobia." He gave a teasing smile. "Night swimming's out."

"I'm fine with that."

He kissed her in the spot right below her earlobe and heat shimmered along her neck. Combine that with the way he rubbed circles in her palms and every nerve ending became sensitive. He gently nibbled on her lower lip making her breath catch. His tongue leisurely flicked against her mouth, and she opened to let him slide in. His mouth came down on hers hard and hot. A needy frantic spike of pleasure streaked up her spine with every stroke of his warm wet tongue. The obvious bulge in his swim trunks proved they were on the same page. The power of her palpable lust hit her, squeezing her lady parts in a way Dr. Arnold Kegel would approve. Yep. She wanted him.

He pulled away. “Sunshine, you’re driving me wild.” He brushed a curl of her hair behind her ear. Staring at her for a suspended moment, his mouth hovered near hers. “Let’s head for the tent.”

Panting, it took several breaths to get out, “Yes, please.”

He swept her up in his arms, reminding her of a romantic movie as he jogged toward the campground.

Don’t fall for him, she told her heart. It had a hard time listening.

CHAPTER 26

Back in Surprise Valley two days later, the sun shone high in the sky as Zack sat next to Birdie on a blanket overlooking the Majestic River. Since this was her last day in town, they'd taken horses and had just finished their picnic.

"I had a great summer." Birdie smiled at him.

"Me too. Since you're a teacher, I think you can relate to this one. In fourth grade, Miss Abbott let me borrow *Moby Dick*. After that, I used to picture myself swimming in the ocean but never got around to it. Thanks to you, I got to swim, bodysurf, and ride a jet ski."

"It wasn't me. Granny and Myrtle planned the trip."

"Yeah. But you were the one I liked watching. You're a natural in the water." Everything she did got his attention.

"You weren't so bad yourself."

"Even when I'm sputtering from a spill?" And she'd circled back to make sure he was all right.

"That's how you learn."

"We have fun together. I hate you're leaving." She'd be in Colorado late tomorrow. "Are you anywhere near Moose Valley?"

"It's about an hour south. Why do you ask?"

"I might be out your way in a couple of months. Maybe we can meet up?"

"Sounds great. Have you been to Colorado?"

"No, but there's a horse breeder I'm interested in seeing."

"It's pretty country. There's lots of open space." She gave a faraway look and took a bite of her sandwich.

"I'm sure you're going to miss Granny."

"We'll FaceTime."

He chuckled at how things have changed. People mailed letters or traveled miles to see people. He had to admit electronic devices held plenty of purpose. Gazing at her face, he said, "You're so pretty."

"So are you." Her eyes shimmered with mischief.

"Thanks, I think." He scooted closer sweeping his tongue along the back of her ear and breathing in her wildflower perfume. God, she smelled good. When he bit her lobe, she actually shuddered under his touch making his cock leap to attention. Dammit. She was going home tomorrow. He'd known it was a fling but somewhere along the way he let himself hope for more. And this would most likely be their last time together. Talk about bittersweet.

But he had her now. He brushed his thumb along her velvety lips. Her mouth opened and he deepened the kiss, reveling in the way her tongue danced against his. They fell back to the blanket with her clinging against his side.

His hands traveled along every inch of her sleek and toned body.

They got lost in a world of touching and stroking, Desperate for each other. Determined to hold onto this moment of being wrapped in each other, this closeness felt necessary. His fingers fisted into her hair.

She rocked against him, grinding multiple times. The heat of his desire made his head swim. The need had their clothes falling off one by one.

He explored, touching every curve as her hands roamed over his body. Biting, licking, exploring. Stirring him up into a frenzy as his hand drifted down to her core and he found her wet. He couldn't resist dipping one finger inside her.

Her body pushed against him, and he added another finger. She let out a little croon, "I want you inside me. Now, Zack."

He grabbed his wallet out of his shorts and produced a condom.

She took it out of his hands, spread it over his stiffening erection, pushed him onto his back, mounting him, and burying his cock deep inside her.

"Birdie," his voice came out a guttural rumble.

She set the speed, slow at first increasing to intense pleasure with each rise and fall of her body. Steady with the motion.

"My turn." He flipped her onto her back, taking control. His hardness pushing against her core.

She arched up as he thrust inside. The friction between them burned like a wildfire.

"Harder, faster," she panted. Her words had him teetering on the edge of release.

He spread her legs wider. His thumb hit her clit and rubbed it.

"So good," she shouted as she spiraled out of control.

He let out his own primal groan as he came. Once he finally caught his breath, he rolled over to his side and pulled her into his arms. He held her as his breathing slowed, all the while wishing this moment could last forever.

"I think we'd better get dressed. I need to shower before the party." She sat up and put on her bra and panties.

He rolled off the condom. "Oh, shit."

"What's wrong?" She asked as she buttoned her blouse.

"The condom broke."

"No worries. I'm on birth control." She stroked her fingers along his arm.

"Thank God." He wasn't ready for a child and released the breath he held, He put on his clothes, moved next to her, and ran his thumb under her chin so she was forced to look into his eyes. "Are we okay?"

"We're fine." She pressed her mouth to him and kissed him.

"Maybe we could have a long-distance relationship." He wanted her to consider him as an option.

"I wish it could work." She looked down at the ground.

"It could be different for us."

"I'm sorry, Zack." She gave a sad smile and shook her head. "You have a breeding program that needs you, while I'm never coming back here to live."

He wanted to argue but could tell she had her mind made up. Unfortunately, he'd already fallen hard for her. He kissed her on the cheek. A deep heaviness filled his chest.

His heart was crushed.

CHAPTER 27

In the old farmhouse, Birdie brushed her teeth in the upstairs bathroom next to the guestroom. Luckily, the location for the party had been changed to the Silver Spur. Originally, Mother intended to have Birdie and Henry's going away party at her parent's house in Oak Hills, but Granny won out. Meaning Mother lost control of the situation.

Imagining her mom sputtering with indignation made Birdie smile.

Mother and she were polar opposites. Mother liked being in control while Birdie considered herself brave, maybe even brazen when it came to trying new things. Hell, she'd done tons of crazy snowboarding tricks, gone river rafting in some of the most difficult waterways, bungy jumped, parasailed, even skydived. She'd thrived in Colorado with its green pastures, majestic mountains, countless lakes, and at least three ski resorts all within an hour's drive.

Still, she couldn't complain about helping Granny recuperate this summer. The woman had always been her rock.

She strode to the vanity in the bedroom, spread out her makeup, swiped a layer of mascara on her lashes, brushed some pink color on her cheeks, carefully applied lipstick, and smacked her lips together.

Then she glanced into the beveled mirror. The same mirror Granny figured had been at the farmhouse for over a hundred years. She wondered how many women had gazed into the same mirror as they got ready for a picnic, shindig, or even a ball.

The grandfather clock in the living room chimed five times.

Better quit primping and get on with the party. She got up, smoothed down the skirt of her dress, and headed down the stairs. A loud din of voices chattered from outside the sliding glass door.

A hand clasped on her shoulder. "Roberta Kellogg, I taught you better manners than to leave all your guests waiting."

"I'm here now and have friends and family to see." She kept her tone steady and firm, stepped out of her mother's hold, and opened the slider.

At least fifty people milled around in the backyard. So

much for a family dinner and a quiet escape back to Colorado. She surveyed the area with extra tables and chairs. Dax and Dawson her twin cousins, Mia's brothers, sprinted toward an open grassy area and threw a football back and forth. A handful of Henry's friends joined them in an impromptu game.

She walked around the yard, stopping to chat with the Brown's who owned an alfalfa farm kitty-corner to the Silver Spur. Their youngest son had taken over last year, and this couple couldn't be "m*ore tickled.*"

"Birdie, partner with me in horseshoes against Dusty and Tyler." Garrett stood next to her.

"You bet. We're gonna cream them."

At one point both teams were tied, but she and Garrett ended up the victors.

"You got your game back." Her brother punched her arm. "It's been nice having you home this summer."

"Like old times." They hugged. "Except now your married."

His smile brightened as he looked over his shoulder. "And here comes Josie."

"That's my clue to mingle." Under the patio awning Auntie Mickie set up a display of cupcakes on a side table while Uncle Al added other dessert platters. Birdie turned and bumped right into Zack. "Sorry."

"No need to be." He grinned. "I was just about to get some food. Wanna join me?"

"Okay." She could eat.

He whistled for Duke, and the dog came to his side.

She reached down, petted him, and was rewarded with a lick on her ear. "Who's a good dog?" She stroked his fur. The lab wagged his tail. "You're lucky to have him."

Zack put his hand on the small of her back and escorted her toward the barbeque and in line behind her youngest brother.

"Hey, Henry. Great party."

"It is." He gave her a lopsided grin, reminding her of the little ten-year-old brother about to snatch a horny toad from underneath a bush.

"You heading for college Monday, right?" Zack asked.

"Yep. We're the smart ones getting out of Dodge." He motioned to Birdie.

"I agree." Like her, Henry preferred to live outside of Surprise Valley.

Her dad and Uncle Aaron manned the barbeque.

"Come over here, shortstop," Dad called. Seconds later she found herself wrapped in a tight bear hug. He smelled like the outdoors and comfort. "I'm gonna miss you something fierce."

"Me, too." Her eyes misted. Dad was her safe haven. Her everything.

"Save some of that hugging for your old uncle."

"You're not old." She squeezed him as she wrapped her arms around his waist.

"Try ancient," Dad laughed.

"Be nice you two." She stepped back and shook a finger at both of them.

"Where's the fun in that?" Her dad set a toasted bun with a burger on her plate. "Medium rare. Specially cooked just for you."

She got up on her tiptoes, kissed his cheek, and headed for the buffet set against the wall, adding watermelon, corn on the cob, macaroni and potato salad, and coleslaw. Zack threw Duke a roll which the dog gobbled down in one bite. She'd miss him and his overzealous dog. Coming home and spending time with Zack hadn't turned out so bad. She'd enjoyed her visit and wished he lived in Colorado. But he didn't. No reason to hope for things that would never happen.

The night continued and she chatted with a very pregnant Mia. Dusty remained by her side occasionally adding in some of his dry cowboy humor. She ate one of Auntie Mickie's cupcakes, had a slice of peach pie, and drank a bottle of Corona.

A flushed cheek Kristy arrived with her boyfriend. "Sorry, we're late. We kinda got sidetracked." Her beaming smile said it all. Clint sat closely with his arm around the back of Kristy.

"No problem." Her friend made it. That was all that mattered.

"Cupid Shuffle" blasted from a speaker.

"You know what that means." Kristy jumped up and tugged on her elbow.

"Dance party." They made their way to the grass and line danced.

Birdie stepped to the left. She kicked forward. "You and Clint look happy."

"I think he might be the one."

"Good for you." Ever since Kristy had been little, she'd dreamed of finding her very own Prince Charming and happily ever after. So far, none of her exes had measured up.

"I think you could have that with Zack."

"If I stayed maybe." But it's time to move on and consider the two months she'd spent with him a fond memory.

The song changed to "YMCA." Her little niece Charlotte tapped her on the leg. "Up. Aunt Bird."

Holding the toddler in her arms, she showed her the motions. Giggles erupted each time the refrain continued.

She and her friends did countless line dances.

"Die a Happy Man" by Thomas Rhett played.

"Wanna dance?" Zack held out his hand and his warm whiskey eyes drew her in.

"Yes, please."

Secured in his arms, his jean-clad thigh pressed against hers. She snuggled closer and got a whiff of his spicy cologne.

"This is nice." He held her tight.

"It is." They kept on dancing like they were the only ones

on the grass. Then the song ended, and she went back to the table.

Dad picked up his longneck and tapped on the bottle with a spoon. Everyone quieted down. "Next week's gonna feel empty around here since two of my kids will be moving on with their lives." He looked in her direction. "Here's to Birdie educating another batch of first graders."

"To Birdie." Everyone picked up their drinks.

"And to Henry, my youngest son. Enjoy college. Just don't forget you're there to learn something."

"I won't." Henry lifted his shoulders.

Everyone toasted her brother.

A COUPLE OF HOURS LATER, her parents were the first to leave. She gave Mother the obligatory kiss on the cheek.

"Call when you arrive in Colorado," Dad said as he wrapped her into a big hug.

"I will."

Granny disappeared into the house leaving Birdie alone with Zack.

"Anything I can do to help you get ready?" Zack asked.

"I don't have much, but you could carry out a couple of things."

"You've got it." His tone came out soft and wistful.

Once they reached her car, she popped the trunk. Her

suitcase fit in vertically and he squeezed in a small box beside it.

He drew her into his arms. His kiss was slow but somehow lacked the vigor she'd enjoyed before. When he pulled away, he said, "Take care of yourself, Birdie."

"You, too."

And then he was gone leaving her a little empty inside.

CHAPTER 28

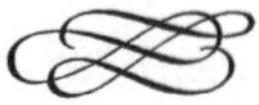

"I'm bored," Birdie sat on the couch thumbing through TikTok animal videos. Usually, they made her laugh but not today. It was her first Saturday home. She had just put her third load of laundry into the washer and already folded the clothes from the dryer. Right now, she just felt blah.

If she'd been out at the farmhouse, she'd text Zack something like a weird science video or a funny meme. She'd gotten used to talking or texting with him.

Too bad he'd wanted to try having a long-distance relationship. She decided to cut all ties with him. It was for the best.

"Let's go horseback riding at the Lucky Eight. We haven't been there in—forever," Ursula said.

"Good idea. Give me a few minutes to change, and I'll be ready."

Twenty minutes later, she and Ursula rented horses and were riding down the trail. She rode a stallion that reminded her of Cinnamon. Her mind conjured up Zack on his steed. Confident. Smiling. Oh, so hunky.

Hells, bells. She had to get him out of her head.

Cisco galloped down the trail toward the river. Surrounded by the picturesque Rocky Mountains made her feel insignificant in its presence. The smell of pine trees filled her lungs with happiness. Just another reason why she loved being outdoors.

"Wait up, Birdie." Ursula yelled. She wasn't the most experienced rider but made up for her lack of skills with enthusiasm.

She slowed to a stop when she reached the water and recalled making love on the hill above the Majestic River. Zack kissing her, stirring her passion with a flick of his tongue. His hands roaming her body, teasing her breasts, dipping his finger inside her center. Her core heated and she squeezed her thighs.

Cisco snorted and walked forward.

Even this steed thought she was being silly.

Ursula trotted next to her, "Race you to the water tower." They always raced. Rentals weren't necessarily the fastest horses, thus the results varied.

"Of course." Today, Birdie got her favorite. Cisco usually did well for her. "On your mark, get set, go." She took off.

Ursula and she were neck and neck as they galloped through the narrow river and up the embankment to the other side where the trail flattened out. It took maybe a few minutes to reach the raised metal tower with a large logo of an upside-down horseshoe with the number eight inside the center.

"I won." Ursula shouted.

"It's a tie," Birdie said knowing she'd been ahead by probably a foot.

"No way. I won fair and square."

"Fine." Birdie decided to give in. After all, she had won every other time they came here. Why not let her friend experience victory for a change? She eased off the pressure of her thighs on her mount. He slowed to a trot, then a walk. This brought her near the skull boulder, the one that creeped her out because it looked like a gigantic skeleton head. As big as it was, the childish part of her brain thought it might swallow her whole. She knew the idea was idiotic still she shuddered at the thought.

Cisco reared. Already freaked about the sinister boulder, she lost her balance. As if moving in slow motion, she tumbled backward to the grassy meadow. This wasn't bad. Not bad at all.

Until her head connected with something hard.

Dots floated in front of her eyes making it hard to see. Then everything went black.

"Birdie, wake up," Ursula called. Fingers pressed against her wrist.

"Are you ladies all right," a male voice said.

"My friend fell off her horse, but she is breathing and has a pulse."

"That's a good sign. Still, I'm going to radio for help."

Birdie recognized that deep voice. "Zack? What are you doing here?" She peeled open her eyes. A middle-aged man in a black Stetson gazed at her. Instead of rich whiskey-colored eyes, this guy had chocolate-colored ones. "You're not Zack."

"Name's Tucker." He looked directly at her face. "Seems you took a fall."

"I did. Where'd Zack go?"

"No one here but this little lady." The guy motioned to Urusla. "And me."

"You've got it bad for Zack," Ursula whispered in her ear.

"I do not." Well, maybe she did. But that part of her life was over. Time to find herself a hunky man. One that wasn't a cowboy living in California.

CHAPTER 29

Zack rode along the trail heading toward the river. Even though it was midmorning, the sun blazed down on him. He removed his hat and wiped away a bead of sweat trickling down his forehead.

Thoughts of Birdie raced through his mind. She'd been gone for three weeks, and he couldn't forget her. He'd been smitten the first time he saw her that Christmas two years ago. And now that he had gotten to know her, he'd kept thinking about the way her green eyes lit up when she smiled. She had this go-for-it-attitude whether she was riding horses or racing past him on a jet ski.

Never in his life did a woman preoccupy so much of his thoughts.

Sure, she lived in another state. For all practicality, he knew a relationship would never work. Honestly, he'd never wanted one before. But this was Birdie. The one he'd been crushing on from the first moment he saw her.

He clicked his tongue and Cinnamon raced along the riverbank. The thrill of speed and the constant beat of hoofs pounding the ground underneath him brought him solace. He basked in the freedom of this open range while his heart felt hollow.

He rode by the fields where they'd picnicked and made love. Forget about her. She's moved on and so should he.

But—he just couldn't.

His horse let out a whinny as he pushed harder and faster along railroad tracks. Cinnamon's hoofs flipped dirt in the air as he galloped along. A locomotive's engine sounded behind him. Something burned against his pocket. Easing up on his reins, he pulled out the red stone he'd found in a field that morning. Unable to drop the object, his fingers clasped around it.

It seemed like some outside force yanked him off the saddle, and he fell toward the tracks and the shimmering light of a locomotive. A rainbow of light twirled in front of him reminding him of a toy kaleidoscope turning round and round.

Dizzy, he closed his eyes.

No wind blew against his face. Wheels clacked underneath the compartment. The back of his seat was soft and cushiony. He took in a deep breath of stifling hot air.

Peeling open his eyes, he looked around a passenger car.

Based on the wide-open windows, the compartment

obviously lacked air conditioning. A cowboy in front of him puffed on a stogie, filling the room with the strong scent. Given the strict laws on smoking in the twenty-first century, no way would this guy be allowed to smoke inside a train.

Then it hit him like a ton of manure. He was in the past.

Shit. Shit. Shit.

This wasn't where he wanted to be. Obviously, fate had other plans for him. He slammed his fist on the arm of his seat.

"Are you all right, sir?" a woman in a long floral dress and matching bonnet next to him asked.

He sucked in a deep breath. Now was not the time to throw a fit. Although that's exactly what he wanted to do.

"Sir?" the woman asked.

"I'm fine, thank you." A newspaper had been discarded on the bench between them. "Are you reading this?"

"No. It's all yours."

He unfolded the page. His eyes drifted to the headline. *"San Bernardino Sun, August 10, 1887."*

Just like Josie, he arrived back to the time he left. How could this be when he'd been in the future for over three years?

He glanced down at his hand. Plenty of callouses. No barbed wire scar on his knuckle when he cut himself at Fairfield Farms. Running his hands on his chin, his beard was short. When he left, he'd been clean-shaven. He could feel the sole of his scuffed boots had a hole near the toe. Plus, he wore denim trousers and a red checkered shirt.

The exact outfit he wore the day he arrived in the future.

"Next stop, Daaaaaaagettt," the porter called.

Right. He'd been heading for his uncle's ranch to help out.

The train slowed and stopped. As if in a daze, he sat there and watched people walk down the aisle.

Get up. He told himself. *This is your stop.*

He made his way to the train's landing. Main Street had a smattering of shops. Less than a dozen people milled by a general store. A buggy parked in front of the livery. The scent of smoky coal from the locomotive combined with fresh air.

No cars. No telephone poles. No electricity buzzing.

Damn. He liked modern technology. The modern era pulled on his heartstrings as did Kristy and her family.

He walked down the steps.

"Over here," someone called. His uncle waved his straw hat. The man in overalls looked so ... well ... old-fashioned.

Aunt Myra rushed over and embraced him with a big hug. Round and full of life, she'd always been his favorite aunt. Whenever she visited, she'd bake the best oatmeal cookies. As a kid she'd always sneak him an extra treat. Maybe she did that for all the kids, but he kept to his illusion that he was her special one.

"I appreciate your help with the drive." Uncle Oliver shook his hand.

Along with his uncle and a handful of wranglers, Zack would help bring several hundred head of cattle to the loading docks outside Daggett. He loved cattle drives.

"How's your ma?" Aunt Anna asked.

"Fine." His mom was still alive. He had to see her. But he'd promised to help his uncle. The internet said she'd die in March. This drive would last less than a couple of months. He still had time to see her.

His aunt smiled. "That's good to hear. Has the cough subsided?"

"Still the same." Soon her illness would kill her. The fact there's nothing he could do had his gut tightening.

"Let's head out to the ranch. The green wagon's mine." He motioned toward the street.

Zack picked up a burlap bag that held his few measly belongings and set it in the back of a buckboard. Helping his aunt onto the seat, he sat next her on the wooden bench. Hard, rigid, nothing like the padded leather seat inside his Mustang.

"Yah," his uncle called, and the horse started walking. Once they got off the main street, his uncle picked up speed.

The same land he'd sped by on the freeway had changed to nothing but sagebrush and creosote bushes and a scattering of cabins along the hillside.

He thought about Kristy and her family. His friends. Birdie. He shouldn't miss her so much, but he did.

Would he ever see any of them again?

It shocked him that he was here and not in the future.

At the moment, he had to accept fate had other plans for him, and accept he was where he belonged.

CHAPTER 30

Birdie's stomach roiled and lurched worse than yesterday morning. She needed to get to the bathroom. Sprinting, she covered her mouth. *Please let me make it.*

She knelt on the cold linoleum floor and wretched. Dammit. She must've caught the flu from one of her students. Good thing it was Sunday and she didn't have to call in sick.

Her roommate, Ursula, knocked on the door. "Birdie, you okay?"

"I am now." Splashing water on her face, she gazed into the mirror. Damn, she looked horrid. Plus, her mouth tasted nasty. Rinsing with water, she brushed her teeth. She walked out and crawled onto her bed, putting a pillow under her head and stretching out.

"I heard you hurl. You catch a bug from your kids?"

"Maybe?" Her students were always passing her their germs.

"It must be a bad one considering you puked yesterday."

"I know."

"Plus, you've been tired the last few weeks. Could you be…." Ursula put a hand on her hip, "preggers."

"No." She shook her head.

"When was your last period?"

"I don't know." She shook her head. "But that doesn't matter. I'm on the patch." Except the patch had been missing right after she got back from Sandy Shores, so she may have been two or three days tops without it. That shouldn't matter, right?

"The patch's not a hundred percent effective. Accidents happen." Ursula gave her a crooked smile. "I could be your honorary aunt."

Her pulse sped through her veins a million miles a minute. "This is just the flu." Nothing more. But if she had the flu, shouldn't she be achy or feverish? After she threw up yesterday, she'd felt great in the afternoon.

Ursula got up and grabbed her purse. "I'm going to the store and getting you a test."

Birdie loved Ursula dearly. They'd been friends through college, but when she got something in her head, she became obsessed. "That's not necessary."

"Yes, it is. Plus, I'll get some crackers and 7-Up. That's good for an upset stomach."

The notion she might be expecting rolled over and over

in her mind.

Carrying Zack's child would be a disaster. She had a life here, one that didn't include him.

She sat there in a funk.

It seemed like hours had passed when the front door slammed. Ursula walked in holding up a paper bag. "Let's get this over with."

"Do I really have to?" She wanted to stay in her bed and hide under the covers forever.

"Yes." Ursula gave her the package, careful to keep her distance.

The box's pink and yellow colors were not uplifting. Instead, a quiver climbed up her spine. Taking the test would be like opening pandora's box.

"Let's do this." Ursula eyed her with her hand on her hip.

The cold bathroom tiles chilled her feet. Her hands trembled as she opened the box and took out a white plastic stick.

"Everything's going to be fine." Her friend said from the other side of the door.

"Easy for you to say." She read the directions. *Remove the cap. Point the tip directly in a urine stream. Recap the device and place it on a clean flat service.*

She yanked her jeans down and sat on the toilet. "Here goes nothing." Several seconds later she was done and placed the stick on the edge of the sink, washing her hands before she walked out.

"How long do you have to wait?"

"Five minutes." She moved into a chair in the living room.

Ursula set the timer on her phone.

"Sure." She was up for anything that would get her to quit focusing on the so-called-elephant-in-the-bathroom. Like waiting for a bomb to go off, each second seemed like an eternity.

Then the timer sounded.

Ursula placed her arm around her shoulder as she led her to the bathroom.

She picked up the stick, covered her eyes with the other hand, and held the stick up to her friend. "I don't want to see. You read it."

Ursula's lips pressed together, and her eyes squinted.

"I'm pregnant, aren't I?"

Ursula nodded.

"This is bad," she cried.

Her friend hugged her. "It's a good thing. You're already great with kids."

"I'm only twenty-five."

"What are you going to do?"

She shrugged. "I don't know. I can't believe this is happening to me."

"There's a reason for everything. From what you've said about Zack, he's a good guy."

Birdie twirled a finger through her hair. Her last night with Zack she had been adamant that long distance romances never work. And he'd looked so sad. If she was being honest with herself, she had been just as sorrowful to see things end.

Could I raise a baby alone? Do I want to be a mom? What am I going to do?

"Call Zack. Let him know the truth."

"You're right." She picked up her phone and called. It rang and rang and rang.

"Hello, this is Zack. You know the drill."

"Great."

"What?" Ursula asked.

"Should I leave a message?"

"Tell him to call you."

"Zack, we need to talk. Call the minute you hear this." She counted silently to ten. Then she texted him.

Birdie: *We need to talk. Call me.*

Three dots spun and spun. She waited and waited and waited.

Maybe he's out of service range. Or maybe he doesn't want to talk with me.

Might as well call Kristy. She got her voice message. Then she texted her.

Birdie: *What's up with Zack?*

Kristy: *He left town.*

Birdie: *Have him call me.*

Kristy: *Can't reach him.*

"What a mess." Tears filled her eyes.

"It'll be fine." Ursula tilted her head and gave a wan smile. "I'll be here for you. Always."

Birdie let the waterworks flow. Damn hormones were already starting.

CHAPTER 31

Present day, December 20

If only Birdie could stay in Colorado with its snow covered mountains and hillsides. The nearby ski resort had over a foot of powder. She loved snowboarding on powder. Too bad the baby crimped any trip up the slopes this winter. In the last two months, she'd come to love him or her.

It was Christmas break. Kristy was working the night-shift, so she rented a compact car to take to her friend's house. God forbid she have her parents pick her up and deal with the wrath of Mother.

And she wasn't ready to meet with Granny. As soon as she walked in the door, her grandmother would smell the endorphins and she would know.

Zack had gone off who knows where and was unreachable. She'd pumped Kristy for info and came up lacking. Still, she hoped he'd return by now. She turned up Buckshot Road and entered the drive toward the Fairfield Farms bunkhouse. Zack's red Mustang was on the driveway.

His Mustang. Yes! He's back in town.

Her heart pounded hard and fast as she parked.

Time to have a heart-to-heart talk with Zack.

Her hands were clammy as she knocked on the front door.

Nothing.

Okay. He's probably at the stables. She strutted down the path. Searching the stables, she found a ranch hand cleaning a stall. "Where's Zack?"

"He went home a couple of months ago." The tall lanky cowboy shrugged a shoulder. "Something about a sick relative."

"But his car's here."

"Didn't take it. Don't know why."

"Thanks." Her stomach churned. Opening the front pocket of her purse, she unwrapped a peppermint and popped it into her mouth.

Now what?

CHAPTER 32

Birdie returned to the bunkhouse, took a leisurely bubble bath, and fell asleep in the tub for half an hour. She put on her most comfortable sleep shirt and tried to binge watch season five of "Outlanders" to no avail. Her brain couldn't concentrate on the characters or the lines or even the pretty scenery. Hungry, she microwaved popcorn only to burn it. The acrid odor still scented the air.

She watched Tik Tok dance videos on her phone. The people were entertaining for maybe fifteen minutes. Right now, she was scrolling social media for anything of interest.

Kristy walked through the door.

"You're home." She rushed over and hugged her friend.

"I'm happy to see you too." Kristy backed up a few steps. "You look different."

"What's up with Zack? I mean, he wouldn't leave his car behind."

"It's a long story." Kristy grabbed a bottle of wine and poured herself a glass. "None for you." She eyed her from top to bottom and plopped down into the couch next to Birdie.

"You know something about Zack. Spill."

"I think Zack's in Cedar Springs. His home."

"Where's that? Oregon? Washington?"

"Not exactly." Kristy crossed her leg and rocked it back and forth. "It's a lot more complicated. Remember when Zack first moved in?"

"When was that? Three or four years ago?" Birdie had still been in college.

"Yep. Well … I told you he was my cousin. That was a lie. The truth is I discovered Zack wandering along Buckshot Road." Kristy looked down. "He—he's from the past."

"Past? What do you mean?" This wasn't making any sense.

"He's a time traveler."

"Quit joking around. This isn't funny."

"No, it's not. Time travel is real." The fact that Kristy's lips didn't quirk up at the corner meant she was stone serious.

"It can't be." Birdie's mouth dropped in surprise. She snapped it closed.

"In 1887, Zack boarded a train in Cedar Springs heading toward Daggett, but somehow ended up departing in Whiskeyville in our time. He walked all the way to Surprise Valley with no horse. No car. Not even a water bottle. His style of clothing seemed odd. Denim trousers tied with a rope belt, a handmade long-sleeved shirt, worn boots, leather hat. And it was August.

She glared at her friend. "Now, I know you're joking." Birdie had done her share of practical jokes so maybe this was payback. Except, Kristy wasn't like that.

"Nope." Kristy sucked in a deep breath. "Anyway, I felt sorry for the guy. So I brought him to my parents, and we took him under our wings. Turned out he fit right in. It made things easier to tell everyone he was my cousin."

Birdie's mind struggled to follow the impossible tale. "I don't get it. How does someone time travel? Do they choose to do it?"

"It's complicated and I'm not the best one to explain it, but I'll try. A portal opens kind of like I've seen in *Dr. Who* or maybe even *Star Trek*. In Zack's case, I don't think it was a choice to go back to the 1800's."

"All right." She nodded, pretending to understand.

"Zack's not the only one I know who went through a portal. Josie did as have others. But I'm getting sidetracked." She waved her hand as if what she just said had no bearing on the conversation.

"What? Now you're saying Josie's also a time traveler."

"She is. Like I said, this whole thing is complicated. There's a lot more to the story which I promise to discuss later. Right now, I'm sticking with the *Sparknotes* version about Zack."

Already confused, she just nodded. This lunacy didn't make sense.

"The best we can figure, a month after you returned to Colorado, Zack went out riding and never came back but his horse did."

"Did you call the police?"

"No. I called Garrett and Dusty. We went out searching for him. He simply disappeared."

"Then, you contacted the police?"

"We couldn't. The authorities might delve more deeply into his identity. This whole situation is tricky."

Zack was from the past. It wasn't logical.

"I know it's a lot to process."

"You think?" Her brain was spinning like a merry-go-round. She breathed in and out. In and out. In and out. "Okay. Let's say I believe you. How do we get him back?"

"I'm not sure. I wish we could wave a magic wand and say abracadabra," Kristy giggled. "I'd do it in a heartbeat if I thought it'd work."

"Of course you would. There's gotta be something we can do."

"Possibly. I'm no expert. You should talk with your Uncle Al." Kristy arched a brow.

"Uncle Al knows about Zack and Josie?" She clenched her hands on the chair's arm.

"And Dusty. He's from the past, too."

"This is way too much to comprehend." Her head beat out a drum solo against her temples.

"Didn't you say Mia was acting weird on that old locomotive trip you two took?"

"She did." Birdie thought back to that day. "Dusty's photo hung in an antique shop's window before we boarded the train. After we passed Whiskeyville, she asked about him."

"She time traveled right before that. Seems she stayed in the past a few months."

"Mia, too? All of this is unbelievable."

"To say the least." Kristy shook her head. "But it's true."

"Will I ever see Zack again?" Her eyes misted. "I came close to calling him when I returned to Colorado after the summer break. Why didn't I call him then?"

"He still would have gone back. Remember it wasn't his choice."

Birdie rubbed her stomach which reminded her of the baby. "I wish I could tell Zack."

"Me, too. But you've got friends and family who will help."

"I can't move here." She shuddered at the thought.

"Just take things a day at a time."

"Think I can skip Christmas Day when I share my news with the family?"

"You'll be fine. There's another Kellogg cousin on its way. Nothing wrong with that."

"I love you." Birdie sat up straighter. With friends like Kristy, she could survive anything.

CHAPTER 33

December 18, 1887

Zack walked up to his parent's ranch house. The green shutters painted his mom's favorite color years ago could use a new coat. The next time he went to the general store, he planned to get some paint for the trim as a surprise. She'd like that. Something to brighten her spirits.

He found Ma alone outside on the porch with a blanket over her lap enjoying the first sunny day in weeks. He'd just finished mucking out stalls and was taking a break.

"Hey, Ma," he sat on the bench next to her. Shadows marred the bags underneath her eyes. In a few months, she would be gone. Not that he could tell her what he knew. "How you doing?"

"Well enough." She took his hand. "What's bothering you,

son. Ever since you returned from Orville's ranch in October, you've seemed lost. Restless."

"I'm chill. Really."

"Chill?" His mom shook her head.

Damn it. He'd just slipped into modern day lingo. "Um … Everything's changing around here." And in his mind he seemed to be straddling two very different centuries.

"What are your plans for the future?" She set her other hand on top of his.

Future. He missed the place every day. But as long as his mom lived, he wasn't planning on going anywhere. "I'm not sure. There's always plenty to do on this ranch, and I like being close to you and the rest of the family. But in reality, Eric inherits this land."

"We Harrisons work the ranch together."

"I know but … Uncle Orville made an offer before I left. He wants me to take over as foreman."

"And that's something you'd consider doing?"

"Come spring I think I'll be moving up there permanently."

"He and Myra would be lucky to have you. Out of all my children, they've always seemed closest to you."

"I feel the same way." They were great. Plus, his aunt and uncle never had any children of their own, so he stood to inherit their land. Unless fate had other plans for him.

His mom started coughing.

He went into the house and poured water from a pitcher into a tin cup and held it up to her lips.

She took several small sips. "Thanks. Doc says I'm suffering from consumption. One of these days, the good Lord will take me."

"I hate that you're ill." And it bothered him that he couldn't do anything to help her. In the future, there were several drugs that could alleviate Tuberculosis symptoms, but they required a prescription. It bugged him that he had no access to the drugs in this century.

"I've lived a good life. Don't fret about me. I've already made peace with my maker." Her eyes sparkled when she glanced toward the sky. His dear mom had plenty of faith which he lacked. "There is only one thing I ask."

"I'll do anything for you."

"Don't forget to save room in your heart for a good woman." She squeezed his hand. "I mean it, Zack."

Too bad only one woman held the key to his heart.

CHAPTER 34

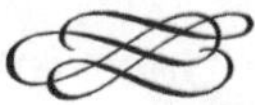

Christmas morning, 1887

Except for the few bouts of coughing, Ma seemed pretty healthy as she sat with the family taking up the third pew. She sang hymns with gusto and said "Amen" countless times during the sermon.

But he could tell the outing took a lot out of her. Her steps were slow as she clung to Pa's arm walking out of the church. And given all the noise coming from the back of the buckboard wagon where most of the Harrisons crammed in shoulder-to-shoulder on top of two rows of haystacks, she didn't turn once to look at any of them.

His oldest sister, Cora, and her husband, and their three children, zoomed past them in their buggy. Being a blacksmith had its perks. His brother picked up the once broken vehicle in exchange for shoeing several horses.

One of his little girls belted out, "Jingle Bells." The song brought back memories of caroling as a kid. The music must be good for the heart because Ma's melodic soprano voice joined in with everyone else.

The wagon stopped right behind the buggy.

"Cora, Ida, Sophia. I need you in the kitchen," Ma called out. "Sarah, take the little ones into the parlor and read to them."

"Yes, Ma." Sarah picked up a toddler in each arm and went inside.

"Pa, please get the men busy." Ma said, commandeering Christmas chores like she had done for as long as he could remember.

He picked up an ax from under the eaves of the house and strolled past venison roasting on a spit over the firepit where the aroma drifted past his nose. His stomach rumbled as he made his way to the chopping block on the other side of the chicken coop. Picking up an ax, he split a log in two, set another log on the block, and split another.

John, his brother came up to him. A year younger than Zack, they'd always been close. "What do you think of this?" He took out a ring with a small garnet in the center.

"Nice."

"Later tonight, I'm gonna ask for Lila's hand." John had been sweet on the neighbor ever since she moved to Cedar Springs last summer.

John rocked on his feet and Zack saw his nervousness.

He'd didn't have to worry. Based on the shy looks Lila gave his brother she was completely smitten with him.

"She'll say, yes." Zack slapped his brother on the shoulder.

John slipped the ring into his pocket, picked up an ax set against a tree, and split a log in two on the second block. "Think you'll ever settle down?"

"I don't know. Maybe." He tried to drone out the idea. He'd always wanted kids of his own.

Pa and Eric took the deer carcass off the spit and started carving the meat on the cutting table.

"Supper should be ready soon. Let's stack this wood and clean up," John said.

Once done, they entered the house his great grandfather had built over a hundred years ago. The original brick fireplace remained in what had once been the whole cabin and now served as the living room. Five bedrooms along with an expanded kitchen and dining room had been added on. Compared to Garrett's parents' home, this space would be considered modest, but for this century it was substantial. His favorite thing about this house—it was homey.

Over twenty people plus kids squeezed into chairs around the table. He scooted into an empty chair in the middle of the back side against the wall.

"Zack, would you say grace?" his mom asked.

He nodded. Cleared his throat. "Lord," he paused. "We honor you on Christmas day. The day Jesus was born. Thank you for our bountiful feast. Our health. Our family. In Jesus' name. Amen."

"Amen," everyone repeated.

Platters of food were passed around. He helped himself to venison, mashed potatoes, baked beans with salt pork and molasses, a vegetable mix of corn, carrots, celery, and chunky applesauce. Ma cooked all his traditional favorites. Sadness lingered in his heart, knowing this was her last Christmas. Next year the family would be broken without her.

"Heard your bull got out last week and caused havoc with your neighbor's stock." John said to Ida's husband.

"Seems he had his eye on the Jones' heifer," Ida snorted.

"It gets worse. The ornery thing not only tore through our fence, but he knocked down the darn outhouse in the process."

"That really stinks." Zack couldn't help adding.

"Amen to that," Pa said with a booming chuckle.

Everyone laughed.

"You still considering heading to the big city?" his oldest brother Eric asked him.

"Uncle Orville offered me a foreman position, but I'm not sure. Maybe I'll go trail riding along the Mexican border." Zack was leaning toward his uncle's ranch ... unless the portal opened up.

"I'm sure you'll figure it out."

Sophia bounced a baby on her lap. She'd been married nearly four years and was already expecting her third child.

They headed for the living room, and he appreciated the spruce in the corner decorated with ribbons, popcorn, and painted dough ornaments. Unlike the trees in the future filled with lights and bling, the simplicity of this tree was nice.

The children were handed stockings filled with peppermint candy, a shiny new tin, and oranges.

Handmade presents were passed out. His nieces hugged their corn husk dolls while his nephews used a string to pull their wooden trains and wagons. Others played with the whittled animals several of which he'd helped carve.

His youngest sister, Sarah, who was now ten, maybe eleven, embroidered him a handkerchief with his initials. He admired the stitchwork and placed it in his pocket. Ma modeled a light blue hat and scarf someone knitted for her. Dad held a handmade shirt against his chest. Others received mittens or socks or embroidered pillows.

They ate gingerbread along with sugar cookies cut in diamond shapes, sang "Joy to the World," "Silent Night," "Jingle Bells," and "Up on the Housetop."

This was one Christmas that would remain in his heart forever.

CHAPTER 35

Present day

It was Christmas morning, and Birdie stared out the passenger window of Granny's Buick Regal.

Thinking back to yesterday, she shook her head. One look at Birdie and Granny said, "You're expecting."

So she spilled. Everything.

Granny didn't judge. She supported her. Always. No matter what happened. She embraced Birdie.

Birdie cried, which wasn't like her. She never used to cry. Not when she got stung by a bee. Not when she broke her arm falling off a motorcycle. Not even when she left her friends and family and moved away.

Stupid pregnancy hormones kept causing havoc on her psyche.

But now as Granny parked the car in front of her

parents', Birdie's pulse sped faster than a race car. She hated the idea of dealing with her mother's condescending looks. One that said, *I knew you'd get knocked up some day. You always chose the hard way.*

"Let's avoid telling your mother until later. I'm not ready to handle the hysterics this early in the morning," Granny said as she took Birdie's hand in hers.

"I agree."

"You'll be fine," she said in a soft, loving tone.

"I doubt it. I don't know if I can face Dad." Seeing the disappointment in his eyes would tear her to shreds. Birdie sucked in a deep breath.

"You're strong. Hold your head high. Another Kellogg in the family is a good thing especially with you as his or her mother."

"Says you." Birdie had plenty of doubts as she glanced down at her bulky sweater, thankful she didn't show. She walked in the front door with a big bag of gifts.

Mother rushed to the entryway. "You made it on time."

Birdie kissed Mother on the cheek and headed straight for the living room putting the gifts under the tree. An eight-foot spruce filled the corner decorated perfectly with red and white crystal ornaments and topped with a blonde angel. No handmade objects. Ever.

When Birdie was in second grade, she'd made a dough gingerbread house with a string on top. Proud of her ornament, she immediately placed it on a limb.

"Sweetie, the tree is for store bought things. Why don't

you hang your art on your bulletin board in your room?" Her mom plucked the ornament off the branch and pushed it into her hand.

From that point on, Birdie never brought her mom anything from school. Not a poem or any of her report cards with straight A's or even a Mother's Day gift.

Her niece tugged on the hem of her top. "Auntie Bird. Let's open presents."

"You have to wait until Henry gets here." April patted her daughter on her head.

Birdie got down to eye level with her niece, smiling into her round face. The girl was cute in a red velvet dress with green striped tights, and red and green ribbons tying up her red pigtails. She pointed to a rectangular box with a doll inside. "This present is from me. You'll get to open it soon."

"Goody." Her niece gave her a delighted little giggle.

"Dad's calling you," April told her daughter.

Charlotte ran toward Tyler, and he placed her on his shoulders.

Birdie's eyes misted. Zack would never be a father to their child, but she'd make sure this baby had plenty of love.

"I need you to take the biscuits from the oven and put them in baskets." Mother pulled her into the kitchen.

"I will."

Her mom got behind her and whispered in her ear. "You're a little chunkier than usual. You might want to cut down on the desserts while you're here."

Leave it to Mother to say something demeaning. Birdie

shook off her irritation, determined not to make a scene. She hadn't been home for Christmas in two years, and this year she had a big surprise. Not bothering with a reply, she filled two cloth covered baskets and set them in the center of the long mahogany table.

"You're here, shortstop." Her dad enveloped her in his arms. "You look as pretty as a picture."

"Thanks, Dad."

Brunch wasn't quite ready, so Birdie moved to a couch in the formal living room next to Mia. "Can I hold Ethan?"

"Absolutely." Mia pushed the three-month-old bundle into her arms.

Birdie admired the cute little outfit and his rosy cheeks that made her want to pinch them. "He's like a mini-Santa."

"I know, right?" Mia scrunched up her nose. "I found that outfit at the mall and had to get it."

The baby's gray eyes were wide and seemed to be taking in his world as he sat on Birdie's lap. "He's so cute."

"We think so." Mia smiled over at her husband who was talking with Garrett by the fireplace.

"You look happy."

"I am. I love being a mom."

"Wait until Ethan starts teething." April moved to an overstuffed chair facing them. "You'll be up all night and most of the next day without a clue how to stop the crying. As much as I love my kids, they are a lot of work."

"Just think, next year this will be you," Mia said softly.

"Excuse me." Wait. Did Mia already know?

Maybe Granny accidentally spilled the news.

No. Granny wouldn't do that.

She turned her head and spotted Josie sitting to the right of her with a rounded stomach.

Whew. Birdie let out the breath she'd been holding. "When are you due?"

"February second."

"Groundhog's Day. Let's hope he or she doesn't see a shadow and stay put for six more weeks." Birdie opted for humor. It soothed her nerves a tinge.

"Not if I can help it." Josie rubbed her stomach.

"Brunch is ready," Mother called.

"Mia, go help yourself. I don't mind holding the baby." Plus, staying put would keep Birdie out of the limelight.

"Thanks." Her cousin walked off with Josie behind her.

Birdie jiggled the baby on her lap. In five months, she'd be holding her own child. Little did she know her trip home last summer would change her life so drastically. At least, she had her roommate. And she'd already started investigating day care. With a few weeks leave from work before the term ended, she'd have the whole summer to figure things out.

Granny patted her on the back as she walked by. Her grandmother's touch calmed her. She rocked the baby on the couch and breathed in his sweet baby smell.

Mia waved her hand in front of Birdie. "You all right?"

"I'm fine." As fine as anyone with a huge secret.

"Get some food. We'll be opening presents soon." Mia took the baby out of her arms.

An hour later, after cleaning up mounds of wrapping paper and boxes, Birdie sat in a chair next to Granny near the Christmas tree. Dusty and Mia cooed with their infant. April and Tyler played on the floor with their little ones. Garrett, Henry, and Dad cheered when their team scored a touchdown on the big screen TV. Mother seemed to hold court with Josie.

Birdie sank against the back of the loveseat.

Granny nudged her and whispered, "Tell them."

The warm air became stifling. She sucked in a deep breath.

Granny squeezed her hand.

Okay. She could do this. Picking up a spoon, she stood and tapped it against her mug of cocoa.

Everyone stopped talking. It felt like hundreds of eyes bored into her.

"I have an announcement." She blinked probably ten times, maybe twenty. She cleared her throat. "I … I'm expecting a baby in May."

Josie clapped. "How marvelous."

Garrett's eyes narrowed, and she thought she heard him murmur, "I'll kill the dude."

Mother paled. Dad's jaw dropped. Tyler cracked his knuckles. April's mouth opened and closed.

Then Henry walked over and hugged her. "Looks like I'm gonna have a little snowboarder to spoil."

"You've got that right."

Mother got up and stood in front of her. "Are you happy

that you wrecked what *was* a wonderful Christmas?"

"I … I," her brain spun around like a hamster in a wheel, trying to come up with the perfect retort. Nothing came.

"Knock it off, Laura," Granny chimed in. "This is something to celebrate."

Her mom stomped into the kitchen which was more than okay with Birdie.

Her father walked over and took her hand in his. "Want to join me outside?" Dad normally had an easy smile. Right now, his mouth dipped down.

Yep, she'd just shattered his view of her. "Sure." She walked with him to the front doorway, grabbed her jacket from the coatrack, and took her usual spot on the porch swing. Plenty of times over the years she sat here with her dad and conversed about anything from how many stars are in the sky to what it was like growing up on the Silver Spur Ranch. They'd laugh and joke and just enjoy the night.

But this was different. If only this were as easy as wishing on a star. Worry filtered through her body and she shivered.

Dad moved onto the bench and put his arm around her. "Seems my little girl's going to be a mother."

"I am."

"Congratulations." His tone lacked its usual jovial quality.

Her heart thudded to a stop. "Thanks." Not about to show her devastation, she flashed him her best smile.

"I have to tell you a baby changes your life. Can I assume the father will be in the picture?"

As much as she hoped Zack to be a part of their child's life, it could never be. "No."

"That's too bad." He lifted a shoulder. "Does that mean you'll be moving home? I really want to watch my grandchildren grow up."

"Probably not." She saw him flinch. "But I … well … the baby and I will come home as often as we can."

"You've always been such a determined girl. Ready to conquer the world." He wrapped his arm around her shoulder and pushed the porch swing in motion. "Just remember I'm always here if you need me. I love you, shortstop."

"I love you, too, Dad." She leaned into him and allowed the rocking to comfort her nerves.

CHAPTER 36

The next morning, Fairfield Farm seemed empty without Zack's presence. Birdie missed his ready smile. His easy-going attitude. His red-hot kisses.

How could she get him back to this time? Sitting on the couch, she sipped her coffee. There had to be something she could do.

Like go after him.

She rubbed her belly. Okay. Not in her condition. What if something went wrong? Medicine back then was pretty barbaric.

Kristy walked into the kitchen and poured herself a cup of coffee.

"It would be interesting to visit the past."

"W-what?" Kristy rubbed her eyes. "Please don't tell me you're thinking about trying to time travel."

"A part of me is curious."

"It is pretty bizarre."

"Baffling is a better word. Mia, Josie, Dusty, and Zack did it." She got up and topped off her coffee. "Did any of them go to another era? It'd be cool if they visited the 1920's like in the movie *Midnight in Paris.* I mean, I wouldn't mind rubbing elbows with F. Scott Fitzgerald or Salvador Dali."

"I agree. The roaring twenties sounded like a lot of fun." Kristy flipped her hair behind her shoulder. "I don't know why but it seems like our time travelers stick to this area in the late 1800's."

"Hopefully, Zack went to his home in Cedar Springs."

"I bet he did."

"I wish I could see him. Talk with him. Laugh with him." Birdie set her cup on a coffee table and sat at the couch.

"So do I. I keep hoping I'll see him walk through the door." Kristy ran her fingers through her hair. "Why haven't you called your uncle? He understands wormholes and portals."

"He was out of town but got back last night. I'll text him now." She nabbed her phone.

BIRDIE*: Think you can come over today?*

Uncle Al: Give me and Mickie an hour.

Birdie*: Sweet.*

. . .

Over an hour later, Uncle Al walked in. "Hey, Birdie." He embraced her in a tight hug.

"I hear congratulations are in order." Auntie Mickie strolled through the door. She opened a cardboard box full of frosted cupcakes with little bows on the top. "The blue ones are chocolate, the pink cherry chip."

"You're the best aunt." Birdie snagged a blue one and moved to the couch. She took a bite. "Yum. You always know just what I need."

"I try." Auntie Mickie set the box on the coffee table and sat in an overstuffed chair.

Kristy reached in for a pink cupcake and seated herself in a recliner.

"Just so you know, Zack's the father." No reason to deny the truth.

"Which leaves you with plenty of questions." Uncle Al sighed and moved next to her on the couch.

"To say the least."

Uncle Al folded and unfolded his hands. "We're not certain Zack went back to 1887 but circumstances point that way. My hypothesis is that he rode along the railroad tracks the day he disappeared."

"Besides his horse arriving back riderless what were the other circumstances?" She crossed her ankle and swung her foot. Back and forth. Back and forth.

"We found his bandana by the railroad tracks."

"The same tracks the legendary ghost train supposedly

haunts?" Since she was a little girl people speculated about the phantom locomotive.

"Yes."

"I've always thought the stories were folklore. You're a scientist. Isn't this hard to prove?" She liked facts.

"What do you know about Hawkin's Projection Conjecture?"

"Time and space are unalterable, so time travel is impossible."

"That's the theory, but I now believe space and time are not static realities. With the right push, time itself could be altered." Her uncle rubbed his chin. "Time jumps—both forward and backward.

"Do space curvatures play into this?" It made total sense to her. Glancing over at Kristy, she had a glazed look in her eyes.

"You are intuitive."

"Just say it. I'm a science nerd." Birdie sat up a little taller.

"Thank God someone understands it. I certainly don't." Auntie Mickie smiled.

"Doesn't matter. Your baking skills are divine." Birdie reached for another cupcake.

Kristy raised her hand. "I know you've tried to explain it before, but I'm still confused."

"Think about space folding in on itself." Uncle Al picked up a napkin and folded it in half. "Where the two pieces come together, they can be bridged and make a portal"

Kristy took the napkin and slowly unfolded it. "So everyone who's time traveled somehow found that bridge where the fold touches."

"Exactly. The two worlds connected." Uncle Al rubbed his chin.

"How does the ghost train come into play? I remember seeing a translucent form right before Garrett went back in time." Kristy jiggled her foot.

"It worked because of a conduit. In our case, garnets caused the dimensions to shift between two places like in the string theory." Uncle Al twirled his gold wedding band.

"I'm starting to understand the concept. Why don't I remember Zack wearing any rings?" Or any other jewelry that Birdie recalled.

"He came to the future with a garnet inlayed pocket watch. Dusty wore a garnet belt buckle. Mia a garnet ring. Josie a garnet necklace."

"You're saying Zack grabbed his pocket watch and chose to go back." The idea that the father of her child was gone forever hurt.

"I can't say for sure. Still, I think he would have told me he was getting the watch. Just so you know, all the jewelry is stored in a cigar box up in Granny's attic." Kristy's brows furled together.

"As a group, we decided it would be best to keep from accidentally opening a portal." Uncle Al rubbed his chin. "Something doesn't quite match up here. I wonder if another gemstone went into play this time. Kristy, you're into geology. What are some local gems found around here?"

"Turquoise, quartz, granite, garnets, and pyrite."

"Remember the fool's gold we found as kids. We thought we were rich when we came back with pockets full of the rocks." Birdie smiled recalling their excitement.

"My dad must've seen our disappointment that we hadn't found gold because he took us out for ice cream." Kristy gave a goofy grin. "I got cherries jubilee."

"I got double chocolate chip." It had been a special day.

Uncle Al cleared his throat. "Can we stick to the topic?"

"Sorry," Birdie shook her head. "We were discussing how garnets aided in time travel, but there has to be more to it. Kristy mentioned riding along the railroad tracks."

"The way I hypothesize this, the combination of galloping which is the momentum along with the garnet create the conduit to open a portal. But this must be done in a precise window of time. In Josie's case, she fell off her horse near the tracks and disappeared right in front of Garrett."

"It sounds like a science fiction movie." Birdie jiggled her foot.

"But way more interesting," Kristy chimed in.

"The people we know have traveled between now and the late 1800's. Plus they stuck to this area. I've been contemplating on this situation. Unfortunately, no theory comes to mind. Not yet anyway," Uncle Al said.

"The idea is pretty amazing. It's hard to believe Mia

ended up going back in time much less marrying the guy from the photo in an antique shop's window."

"Her love saved him. Dusty walked along the railroad tracks on his way to the gallows …" Auntie Mickie pressed her lips together.

"Gallows. Like hanging." Birdie had teased her cousin about the man's demise.

"He came close," Uncle Al added. "Somehow he managed to get away and board a train to the future and Mia."

"It's as if fate was playing matchmaker," Kristy simpered. "When Josie returned back to her time. Garrett insisted we attempt to retrieve her."

"Actually, we assumed Zack was the logical choice to go after Josie since he'd been there before. He made several attempts, but it wasn't until Garrett gave it a try that the portal opened." Uncle Al shook his head.

"That's because Garrett admitted he loved Josie right before he left." Kristy put her hand over her heart. "To make a long story short, Garrett rescued Josie and they got their happily ever after."

"It's so romantic." Auntie Mickie fanned her face.

So much for Birdie asking someone else to go back and retrieve Zack. Love played into all of this.

Did she love Zack?

Her pulse quickened. Her heart fluttered way too fast.

A sure sign of love.

Then the baby kicked.

She loved this baby.

Uncle Al hugged her. "If it's meant to be Zack will find his way to you."

His handsome face came to mind. Would she get another chance with him?

CHAPTER 37

March 4th, 1888

Everyone in town crowded around a mound of dirt where his mom's coffin would rest for eternity. Snow flurried on the gravesite. Later this afternoon, a substantial storm was supposed to hit. No matter the cold, people of Cedar Springs came to pay their respects to the woman who had lived in this community her whole life.

The distant snowcapped San Bernardino Mountains seemed like silent witnesses to this somber day. Standing between his brothers, Zack pulled up his collar, trying to ward off the chill that also numbed his fingers.

Dark ominous clouds threatened to blanket the ground with more snow. He didn't mind. Every snowflake was like Ma saying her final goodbyes from the heavens.

As sad as her death had been, peace filled his soul. He got

a chance to see her again. Spend time with her. Tell her one last time how much he loved and appreciated her.

Yep. He was mighty thankful.

Boot steps crunched as the preacher took his place at the far end of the grave. The man tightened his woolen scarf around his neck and cleared his throat. "Dearly beloved." His breath puffed out the words like a stream of smoke. "We are gathered here today to pay tribute to Virginia Margaret Harrison, our departed friend, mother, grandmother, and wife. Virginia was a God-fearing woman. Always one to help a friend in need." The preacher folded his hands together. "She now rests with our Almighty Lord."

He paid little mind to the words of the service. A part of him felt melancholy because he'd never again see her.

The air turned frigid, and he fought to keep his teeth from chattering. It didn't take long for his pa, brothers, and him to pick up shovels and pile dirt over the graveside.

A slate headstone carved by one of the townsfolk was placed on top of the mound.

His sister, Cora, cried into a handkerchief while her husband wrapped his arm around her shoulders. Next to her, Sophia comforted Sarah. Ma had always been such a force in everyone's life.

John placed his hand on Zack's shoulder. "At least she isn't suffering any longer." His brother's eyes etched in sorrow.

"She'll remain in our hearts."

"That she will." John's lips pressed together. Lilly walked

up placing her arm on his shoulder. His posture relaxed. With his fiancée at his side, his brother's sadness softened, and he eased into her touch.

The rest of the day slipped past. Folks stopped by the house to give condolences and bring food.

Needing to get away, he stepped into the stable. His father stood at the second stall feeding grain to his mom's horse, an old appaloosa. "Reckon you miss her just as much as I do," he said to the animal.

Zack walked up to his dad. "We all miss her."

He got a faraway look in his eyes. "I've known Virginia most of my life. Went to school with her."

"She said you once stuck the end of her braid in an inkwell."

"Had to figure out some way to get her attention. It worked in getting her riled. Over the years, I've learned it's best to keep her happy." The corner of his lips lifted. "Or at least I tried my best. Gave her a roof over her head. Made sure she was provided for."

"You did a good job. When did you start courting her?"

"Not 'till I turned sixteen. Spotted her wearing a green dress at the spring barn dance sipping punch with one of my sisters. Her blonde hair pulled back in a ribbon. And when she looked my way, she smiled." The appaloosa whinnied, and his dad rubbed his hand along the horse's muzzle. "Then I marched up to her and asked her to dance."

He tried to imagine his dad as a young man. Dressed in

his Sunday best. Probably wiry, skinny, and standing tall as he spoke with her.

"Asked her to marry me a year later. Built her a cabin overlooking the river." Pa's eyes crinkled. "Lived there three years until your Gramps died and we moved into the big house. Expect I'll miss her till the day I die." He wiped at his eyes.

"She was the best."

His dad nodded. "Reckon you'll be heading out for Orville's soon."

"I'll be boarding the train tomorrow." He'd been grateful to come home and reconnect with his family. While his relatives could be bossy and overwhelming, he loved each and every one of them. His sisters lived on neighboring farms, ranches, or even in town with their husbands. His older brother built a home for his family up on the hill. John courted the Johnson girl and would probably be married before harvest season. He already had a passel of nieces and nephews he adored. Everyone was busy with their own lives.

It was time to start a new life—whatever that might be.

"I wish you well." His dad hauled him into a bear hug, something he rarely did. And it felt damn good.

CHAPTER 38

Zack boarded the train that stopped on the outskirts of Cedar Springs. If he had his way, he'd make it back to the future. If not, he'd end up at his uncle's ranch. Whatever happened, he'd accept his fate.

He took a window seat in the third row from the front behind a man wearing a Derby. The man lit up a pipe. Smoke curled, filling the passenger car.

Needing fresh air, he opened a window. Pulling the stone out of his pocket, he rubbed the garnet. It still baffled him that he found it on the ground inside the stable. Al had said garnets were a catalyst. A catalyst to open the portal.

The porter shouted, "All aboard!"

The train lurched and wheels clacked from underneath his open window. He gazed out to the Mohave River meandering by pastures and ranches and farmhouses. Horses and cattle grazed on the hillside. They climbed the Cajon Summit and passed Oak Hills Loading Station. In less than an hour he'd be in Daggett. Maybe pick up lunch in town and head over to his uncle's ranch before nightfall.

Unless … he ended up lucky again. When he, Josie, and even Garrett traveled forward in time, they all boarded a train.

The train went up another hill, around the curve, and past the mortuary on the outskirts of Hesperia.

A soft humming filled his ears and added to the excitement buzzing through his veins. He stroked the garnet with his fingertips. The stone burned hotter as he rubbed back and forth. Back and forth. Back and forth.

The room spun with a rainbow of colors. Swirling faster and faster. Making him dizzy. Forcing him to close his eyes as the train's brakes screeched.

The signs are here. *Please let this work.*

He closed his hand around the stone and used his other fingers to hold the side of the seat to keep from falling.

This reminded him of another time on a train.

The motion stopped, and he was afraid to open his eyes. Afraid to hope this wasn't just an illusion. Afraid to be disappointed.

But he lifted his lids and looked around. Chilled air blew in from the vents above. The low back seats had been replaced with high back ones. This was a modern train.

Yes! He'd made it to the future.

All noise was muffled. His limbs were heavy, paralyzed.

A voice from above called, "Whiskeyville Station."

People stood. Three teenage boys walked to the isle, each one glued to their cell phones. The cargo shorts and T-shirts and flip-flops were a far cry from the clothing in the nineteenth century.

Amazed to be here, he couldn't stop smiling. He practically skipped down the metal stairs and onto the Old Town Whiskeyville's platform.

Glancing across the street, a handful of tourists ambled in front of the general store. People milled around the depot. Looking through the window display, it featured old rusted tools. Old in this century. New in his. Given the fact the boardwalks weren't packed, he assumed it must be a weekday.

A memory flashed into his mind. Garrett met Josie in this very spot. He'd mistaken her for the mayor's daughter and was supposed to fake arrest her for a fundraiser. Only the mayor's daughter didn't show, and Josie landed here from the past. A year later, Garrett proposed to her.

Zack had hoped for a love like theirs. An image of Birdie and her kick-ass attitude came to mind. Not the time to be thinking of her.

He should be doing something else like heading back to the bunkhouse.

His phone should still be in his bag. He sifted through his

clothes and felt it at the bottom, got it out, and clicked the side. It remained black.

Dead.

As if he should have expected it to work. It hadn't been charged in months or more like hundreds of years.

Now what? He sat on a bench. *Borrow a cell from someone.*

The people rushing past didn't even look at him.

An older gentleman with a cane eased next to him. "You okay, son?"

"I would be if I could call my cousin. My cell died."

The man reached into his pants pocket and handed him a flip-phone "Help yourself."

Luckily, he'd memorized Kristy's number and punched it in. "Hello. This is Zack."

"OMG. You're back. I mean, I hoped you'd return but didn't think I'd ever hear from you again." Excitement shrilled her voice as she bombarded him with incessant talk, and he figured she'd be bouncing on her toes.

"Look. I'm on a borrowed phone at the Whiskeyville Station. Would appreciate a ride."

"I'm at work but don't worry. I'll find someone," she said.

"You're the best. I'll wait in the front parking lot." He let out a long breath and handed the phone back to the man. "Someone should be coming soon. Thanks."

"You're welcome. Have a nice day. I know I will." The old man whistled as he headed toward a couple with two young kids.

Strolling east on the boardwalk past the depot, Zack walked by souvenir booths on the sides of the dirt path and made his way to the parking lot taking a bench that faced the road.

Cars and trucks zoomed fast on the street filling the air with exhaust. Who knew he'd miss all this chaos? He couldn't wait to drive his Mustang or get on a horse and race along the river in this modern world.

A truck pulled into the parking lot and Garrett got out.

"You're here." Zack held out his hand.

Garrett punched him in the stomach slamming the air out of his lungs.

"Umph," Zack groaned. "What the heck?"

"That's for knocking up my sister."

"What are you talking about?"

Instead of answering his question, Garrett strode to his truck, forcing Zack to run in order to catch up. Garrett clicked the doors open and got in.

Zack strapped into the passenger seat.

"Birdie's pregnant."

"What?" His breath hitched.

"She's having your baby dumb ass." Garrett clenched his jaw. "I mean, she never told me who's the father, but I did the math and figured it had to be you."

This couldn't be right. Birdie was on birth control.

He couldn't think. His hands got clammy. His chest became unbearably tight.

Birdie was having his baby.

Wait. That's a good thing. He'd been in love with her from the moment he met her. Last summer had been fantastic because of her. She made little things like eating ice cream or going on a picnic fun. They clicked in all the right ways.

The baby made a perfect reason to be together.

"You slept with her, right?" Garrett grumbled.

"Well, yes."

"What are you gonna do?"

"Marry her." That's what honorable guys did. "I can build us a house on my uncle's farm."

Garrett laughed. Not just a chuckle. He laughed hard and deep. "You think she'll move back to Surprise Valley?"

"Why wouldn't she? Her family's here."

"Have you met my sister?" Garrett eyed him sideways. "She's stubborn. Everyone has tried to talk to her. Granny guilted her with her heart condition. Kristy promised to help her. Even my dad begged, and you know how she adores him. But she's got it in her head that this baby will grow up in Colorado." Garrett turned toward him and pushed up his sunglasses. "What are you going to do about it?"

"I don't know." His head was still reeling from time travel. "Go after her."

"And then what? Throw her over your shoulder like a neanderthal and drag her back here?"

I'm gonna be a father. He had to figure out what to do. While they were together, she may have considered him a summer fling, but he always wanted more. "I want to make this right not just because she's pregnant but because I love her." That was the first time he said he loved her out loud. And it felt damn good.

He'd made it back where he belonged. And if he were lucky, he might just capture Birdie's heart.

CHAPTER 39

Well after six p.m., Birdie rubbed her neck, rolled her shoulders, arched her back, and leaned back into the couch.

"Long day?" Ursula plopped next to her.

"You don't know the half of it." Wednesday mornings were collaborations with colleagues; thus, her day started an hour earlier than usual. Normally, she loved those days because she got out early. But not today. She was stuck in meetings doing Individual Educational Plans for three of her lower performing students, each lasting an hour. Add in the pizza she ate for lunch, which landed her with heartburn, and she decided being seven months pregnant sucked big time. And she still had two more months to go.

"How 'bout I make you a cup of tortilla soup and you can tell me about it?"

"I'd love that." Her stomach rumbled as she got up and took a chair at the kitchen table. "It's been a long day."

Minutes later, they both had steaming soup and French bread slathered with butter in front of them.

"Any news about the promotion?" Her roommate was hoping to get the manager position at a restaurant where she worked.

"Not yet." Ursula crossed her fingers.

"They'd be idiots not to move you up."

Her little girl decided to kick at her ribcage like a soccer player trying to score. "I love you, sweet pea." She put her hand on her stomach. "But could you be a bit gentler please?"

As if the baby heard her, she kicked even harder.

"Ouch," Birdie laughed as she winced in pain. "I have a feeling this girl is going to come out running full force and never stop."

"Then it's a good thing you've got running shoes."

"Knowing how active she is, you'd better get out your own sneakers because you'll be helping me run interference with the baby."

"Anytime." Ursula gave her an that's-what-friends-are-for smirk. "I'll get the dishes."

Birdie moved to the couch, more than ready to relax.

Someone gently tapped on her door.

"I'll get it," Ursula called.

"Is Birdie home?"

Birdie recognized Zack's deep baritone voice. What in the world? Her heart thudded to a stop.

"How can I help you?'" Ursula asked

"I'm Zack Harrison ... um ... Fairfield."

"The same Zack Birdie's been looking for?" Ursula's tone rose a notch higher.

"Yep."

Zack's here? It couldn't be true. She assumed he had remained in the past.

His tall frame filled the entryway, and he stepped into the living room eyeing her from top to bottom and stopping at her belly before flicking to her face. "Hello, Birdie." His lips quirked up at the corners. "These are for you." His hands shook slightly as he offered her a bouquet.

She understood his hesitancy because she had her own. She'd never expected to see him again. And now with her situation, well ... She sniffed a pink carnation. and sighed, "Thanks."

"May I sit?" He motioned to the empty spot on the couch next to her.

"Of course." Her eyes caught with his. And holy hell, she missed him.

"You two need to talk." Ursula picked up her keys from the counter. "I'll be back in a couple of hours."

The front door shut leaving her alone with the father of her child. She waited for him to pull her into his arms and kiss her. Say he'd missed her. Ask about the baby. But all he did was put his hat in his hands and spin it.

Hiding the longing in her heart, she asked, "What happened? I thought you went back to the 1800's."

"I visited my family. Left the day after we buried Ma."

"I'm sorry." She placed her hand over his, hoping he'd entwine their fingers or show a hint of what he was thinking. "That must've been rough."

"At least I got to say goodbye." He closed his eyes.

He'd been through so much. "How'd you make it back to our time?"

"Right after Ma died, I boarded a train and was sucked through the portal." He gave her a lop-sided grin. "Garrett punched me in the gut and told me you were carrying my child."

"Sounds like him." That stung. She had been missing him, and all he cared about was the baby.

"Can't blame him being protective of his little sister."

"I know." All her life, her three brothers watched out for her.

"Did you know about the baby when you left Surprise Valley?"

"No. I found out late September. I called. Left dozens of texts."

"Shit. I was thinking about you when I stumbled into the past.

Her heart thudded a little faster.

"I missed you." He took her hand in his and kissed her knuckles

Her pulse sped up. "We can't change what happened." The baby booted her side. "Ouch."

"Are you okay?" His eyes squinted in concern.

"Fine. It's the little one. Wanna feel?" She took his hand and brought it to her stomach. "She is quite active."

"She. We're having a girl?" his voice rose.

"Yes. How do you feel about becoming a father?"

"I'm hell-fired up. Ready to do a jig or jump over the moon. This is my daughter." With his hand on her stomach, the baby kicked. "Does she know I'm here?" His whiskey eyes lit up.

"She knows someone is near me." Or she was just restless, but Birdie chose not to ruin his enthusiasm. Then the baby kicked again.

"Our daughter's wonderful."

"She is pretty special." Birdie put her hand on top of his.

"I want us to be a couple."

Her heart said yes. Maybe they could make this work. Her conscious warned her he might only want her because of the baby.

"Would you consider moving back to California with me?"

And just like that, all those warm fuzzies blew away. Anger burned through her veins. He thinks I'm going to live in the same town as my mom. Hell, no. "You don't know me very well to ask that."

Apparently, he never picked up about my relationship with Mother.

"What?"

How dare he act all innocent with his wide eyes and surprised expression. Her blood pressure must've spiked.

"I told you at the end of last summer this is my home. I'm raising my child in Colorado." She poked him in the chest. And she thought she loved him? Right now, she didn't really like him.

"Our child."

She couldn't do this with him. Not right now. "I'm tired." She slumped into the couch.

"I want to be in both of your lives."

His tone sounded sincere, but after suggesting she upend her life and move back to California, she didn't want to have this conversation with him. "I've had a rough day. You need to leave." Her energy drained to totally exhausted.

"Please, Birdie. Let's talk this out."

She walked to the door and opened it.

"Please don't do this."

She wouldn't even look at him as she motioned to the door. Once he was gone, she leaned against it. "I'm never going to live in California—ever."

Then the waterworks began.

Her stupid hormones had her acting a little crazy, but she was too exhausted to care.

CHAPTER 40

Zack woke up at the Hampton Inn where he'd booked a room for the week. Forcing his eyes open he raked his fingers through his hair. All night he'd tossed and turned dreaming about Birdie and his baby.

What was wrong with him? He knew she didn't want him. Would never want him for anything more than a summer fling. Still, he couldn't walk away from his child.

His phone chirped. and he picked it up from the nightstand.

Birdie: *Can we talk?*

Birdie: *Meet at a coffee shop at 4?*

Zack: *I'll be there.*

. . .

He had a chance to turn things around and needed time to come up with a plan.

At three forty-five, Zack waited in a booth inside Daybreak Diner facing the entrance while tapping his fingers on the table. The door opened and in walked Birdie wearing an oversized shirt that showed off her rounded belly. Her face glowed as her eyes darted until they found his. She bit her bottom lip obviously nervous about their meeting.

She wasn't the only one.

"Hi," she struggled to slide into the booth across from him. "Thanks for coming." Her words came out clipped.

Like he wouldn't be there. "This is important." How he wished he could reach across and grab her hand. Better yet, kiss her senseless. But he could tell she wasn't ready for his touch.

The waitress came by and refilled his coffee. "You ready to order?"

She picked up the menu. "I'll have a hamburger, fries, and herbal tea."

He ordered the same, and the waitress scurried off.

Silence followed. As if they were virtual strangers who'd just met for the first time. God, he hated this. Usually, they would be joking around, laughing, talking about everything from the newest sports car to what movie is the best.

"I don't want to be a part-time dad. I want a family. I

want to be there." He broke the quiet. There. He said it. His gut tightened with angst.

"I want us to be a family too." She blinked and cleared her throat.

Yes. Now to fix their misunderstanding yesterday.

"It's just that I can't go back … to California."

"Why not?"

"There's a lot of reasons, but the main one is my mother. You know we're not close."

"I've noticed." Whenever the two of them were in the same room, the friction had been like a firecracker ready to explode. Still, this was her mom.

"When I was a little girl, I really did try to be the daughter she wanted. I went along with Mother's insistence I participate in beauty pageants which made her ecstatic." She fiddled with her napkin. "On the day of the competition, she'd act sweet. Dolling out attention like I were the best child ever."

The waitress brought out their food. He dipped his fries in ketchup and took a bite, giving her as much time as she needed to continue.

She sipped her tea. "I despised dressing up. The caked-on makeup. The false eyelashes. The high heels that were hard to walk in. Don't get me started on the talent contest. Mother put me in dance classes. My tap routine was mediocre at best, much to her dismay." Birdie's mouth pinched together. "She didn't get that I'd rather be outside looking for insects, riding motorcycles, or galloping on the back of a horse along the river."

"You are quite the adventurer."

"I've always been that way. Dad understood. He encouraged me." She nibbled on her toast. "The problem was he wouldn't stand up to her. I was the only daughter and Mother had dreams for me. Too bad those dreams hadn't included my wishes. Do you know how hard it is to never be loved for me, for who I am? I'll never be the daughter she loves. I don't measure up to her standards."

Zack thought about his ma. She might have been stern and strict. Still, she only wanted what was best for him and his siblings. This woman fanatically attempted to control her daughter's every move, and he'd been oblivious to how the actions affected Birdie. "That's plain wrong." He reached across and took her hand.

"You think?" She lifted a shoulder. "Anyway, when I finally rebelled and refused to enter any more contests, Mother called me ungrateful."

"Now I get it." He threaded his fingers with hers. "You equate going home with tons of bad memories."

"Not for a short-term visit, especially when I stay with Granny." Her eyes sparkled when she said her grandmother's name. "It's just when I'm in Colorado, I'm free from Mother's expectations."

"I'm the one who's sorry now." He'd been determined to regain the woman he loved and didn't understand why California held such traumatic emotions for her. "Just so you know, I asked you if you'd consider moving back. I would never force you to do anything."

"To be fair, I'm hormonal. One little thing can set me off. Yesterday, it was you." She let out a long breath and smiled. A beaming smile that lit up her eyes to a shade of deep emerald. And then her mouth dropped.

"Okay. That makes sense. Kind of," he laughed. "And you're more beautiful than ever."

"I'm as big as a whale."

"Hardly." He wished she were sitting next to him because he longed to touch her. "I still can't believe you are carrying my child. I bet our daughter will be as beautiful as her mother."

Birdie's cheeks flushed making her even prettier.

"There's still the problem of you living in California and me in Colorado." Her brow rose.

"We'll work something out." What? He had no clue.

CHAPTER 41

Friday around noon, Zack lugged a big box from the car.

Ursula rushed from her chair on the porch and led him through the gate to the backyard. "You should set up on the grass under the tree."

Somehow, he'd managed to get the roommate on board with his surprise. "I'm glad you're okay with all this."

"Birdie's like a sister to me. Promise you'll treat her right." Ursula wagged a finger at him.

"I can't say we won't ever fight. I'm a cowboy through and through which means I can be plenty ornery." He tipped his Stetson. "But I'll try not to ruffle her feathers too much."

"Deal." Ursula held out her hand and he shook it.

He opened the box and poured out the parts. "Please tell me you know how to put this mess together.

She gave him an impish smile. “Pop-up tents are a piece of cake.”

“I thought it’d be easier. It’s not.” While he lay the tarp out and figured where the top was, she spread out the other parts.

“I thought most guys love to figure out directions.”

“Not me.” He’d planned to look the directions up on You Tube but ran out of time.

Ursula sat on her knees. “Help me thread these poles through the center. Then we can set the stakes.”

In a few minutes, he had shelter. Then he went to the car to get everything else. Three hours until he either had the woman he wanted, or he’d be heading back to California alone.

BIRDIE PULLED into her driveway dead tired from a long day of kids screaming and the fact she hadn’t gotten one bit of sleep because of the baby. Normally, she’d stay an extra hour to straighten up her classroom and get ready for her next week, but today she just didn’t have the energy.

She opened the door and spotted Zack sitting in a recliner scrolling his phone.

“I thought we were going to dinner later.” She hadn’t seen him since the coffee shop. They still had so much to discuss.

“Change of plans.” He got up and wrapped her in his arms. “There’s a surprise for you in the backyard.”

"What is it?" She snuggled into him, breathing in his masculine scent.

"That would take away the fun." He wore a cat-that-ate-the-canary grin.

"Just tell me. I hate surprises."

"Sorry. No can do."

"This better be worth it." Curiosity won out. That and the fact that his hand on the small of her back created warm tingles up her spine. Holy moly, the guy's hard to resist.

Cracking the door, Michael Bublé's, "Unforgettable," blasted from a tent.

"I love this song."

"That's because you're unforgettable, sunshine." He moved his hands to her shoulders and crooned into her ear.

Sunshine. His nickname for her. One that reminded her of flowers and trees and being outside. Her heart skipped happily in her chest. She managed to step down to the backyard and that's when she spotted rose petals leading a path to a tent. "W-what's this about?"

"Showing you how much you mean to me." He led her to the tent and unzipped the front panel. Blankets and pillows covered a blow-up mattress. Following her inside, he plucked a rose from the center and handed it to her.

Bringing the flower to her nose, she inhaled the sweet fragrance. "Think you could help me sit? I'm not as agile as I use to be." She motioned to her belly.

His eyes roved over her from stomach to face. "You're

beautiful." He held her hand as she eased onto the air mattress. It was as if she floated on a cloud of covers. She plumped up a pillow behind her, leaned back and thought about closing her eyes but nixed the idea. If she did, she'd probably fall asleep.

He eased in next to her. "I thought about what you said yesterday. It baffles me that your mom could be so mean."

"You aren't the only one."

"I finally get why you can't move back. From what I've seen of this town, we could make a nice life here." His eyes met hers. "As long as I have access to horses and wide-open spaces, I can survive anywhere."

It would be easy to fall into his arms and believe this was meant to be. If only she could shake off that niggle of doubt clouding her thoughts. "Why?" she had to ask. "Because of the baby?"

"That's an added perk. One I didn't even learn about until Garrett picked me up at the train depot. It's not the reason I want to be with you. Need to be with you, Birdie. I love you." He took her hands in his.

It was as if the earth quit rotating and abruptly stopped. Everything in the world ceased to exist except for the two of them. "You love me?"

"Yes. I think I fell in love when I laid eyes on you that first Christmas you came home. You marched into your grandmother's farmhouse wearing a red sweater dress and beamed when you spotted your dad. Then you flitted around the room, hugging everyone, kissing your little niece on the cheek, bringing sunshine to everyone in the room like a sun goddess, and damn if I didn't want to be a part of your brightness." His thumb ran circles around her palms causing little crackles and sparks where they touched. "But you didn't even notice I existed."

"That's where you're wrong. I thought you were good looking even from a distance." She yanked her hand away and folded her fingers together. "What good would acting on my attraction have done? I'd be leaving in a few days and didn't plan to come back anytime soon. Thus, I acted polite."

"We weren't meant to be back then." He kissed her cheek.

Her heart pitter-pattered.

"When I was in the past, you were always there. When I went out riding, I'd remember us racing along the wash. When I swam in the river, I thought about our trip to the ocean. When I slept, I dreamed of you. Night and day you were always on my mind." He pulled her into his arms.

Feeling his body against her was wonderful.

As if Zack planned it, Willie Nelson's song, "Always on my Mind," played. Her throat tightened, and she swallowed hard. Tears rolled down her cheeks as she kissed him.

His mouth was on hers, showing her with the sweep of his tongue and the way he held her how much he truly cared. They kissed for the longest time, neither one of them wanted to break the spell. They finally broke for air.

Then he was next to her, taking her hand in his and

moving down on one knee and removing a black box from his pocket.

Her pulse skittered through her veins, and she couldn't help smiling. This was like a romantic movie.

"Fate brought us together for a reason." His hand trembled slightly as he held her. "Will you make me the happiest man on earth and marry me?"

Zack wanted to marry her. Should she take the chance?

"What do you say?"

"You really don't mind moving to Colorado?"

"Not at all." He kissed her forehead. "Please, say yes." His warm whisky eyes showed worry.

She loved him, and he loved her. They belonged together. "Yes, Zack."

He slipped a ring on her finger, pulled her onto his lap and kissed her long and hard and full of hope. "I can't wait to make you Mrs. Zackary Harrison."

"You mean Harrison-Kellogg."

"You're always full of surprises. One of the many things I love about you." His mouth covered hers again.

"What's up with the tent?" She suddenly had to know.

"The first time I got to hold you in my arms all night long, it was in a tent at the beach."

"Such a romantic." Then she thought about that night. "If I recall clearly, the pup tent was rather cramped."

"I'd call it cozy. Although, I opted for more room this time." He feathered kisses along her neck.

"Good choice."

"There's another reason for me setting up camp here." He cupped his hands around her cheeks and pressed his forehead against hers. "The tent is a place for me to hang my hat and prove I'm staying in your life. If you'll let me, I'll always be nearby."

They made love in a tent full of promises.

CHAPTER 42

The next morning, Zack woke up inside the tent with Birdie's warm body curled around him. Her baby bulge pressed against his stomach. Her hand rested on his waist. Her eyes were closed.

Joy soared through his heart. He held the woman he loved beyond time. They were soulmates. Destined to be together.

Her body stirred, and her lashes fluttered opened. She gazed into his eyes, and he fell in love all over again. "Morning, fiancée." He took her hand and caressed the knuckles one by one.

"Hey." She arched against him wrapping her arms around his neck. "It's nice waking up like this."

"It is." She held up her hand and stared at her ring. "I love you, fiancé." The three little words slipped out easily.

"I love you, too." He brought his mouth to her in an exquisite, tender show of how happy she made him. He traced circles along the mound which held his precious child. Lightness filled his chest at the idea of becoming a father. "We're having a baby. I still find that incredible." Happiness soared through his soul.

"I wonder if our baby will have your eyes or mine?"

"Since it's a girl, her gorgeous green eyes will be just like yours." He pictured Birdie holding their child wrapped in a pink blanket.

"And I think she'll have whiskey-colored eyes and a wicked grin. Driving all the boys wild." Her lips pressed into a serious line. "I wish you'd been with me when I told my family."

"So do I. How bad was it?"

"Horrible. At least I had Granny, otherwise, I would have totally lost my bananas."

"Lost your bananas?" he laughed.

She slapped his hand. "Anyway, the next morning I considered the possibility of chasing you through time. I figured I'd slip back in time for a few days. Once I saw you again everything would be settled."

"You did?"

She nodded. "The problem with that idea was the risk involved for our baby. And there was the time variable along with no guarantee I would end up in the right year. So I might be in another century pregnant and alone. Stuck with no way to return."

"But you thought about it?"

"Yes. Still … what if I made it safely to you and … you weren't happy to see me?"

Zack drew back in surprise. "You never have to worry." He brushed his lips against hers. "I'm always happy to see you."

"Such a charmer." She gazed at him with tenderness.

"Only with you, sunshine." He caressed her cheek.

Her fingers laced through his hair and tugged him forward. One of her legs wrapped around his thigh so her rounded belly pressed against him, and she angled her jaw and brought her soft velvety lips against his.

He registered the warmth of her mouth. She ran her tongue along the seam, and as she bit his lower lip any serious thoughts vanished.

His body vibrated with longing. He captured her mouth with more urgency.

The pads of her fingers lightly caressed the hairs on his chest. Her touch continued down to his abdomen and stopped at the top of his boxers. Tormenting him even further she kissed him with an intense hunger that brought his cock to immediate attention. "You like that?"

"I like everything about you." As much as he wanted to bury himself deep inside her, he wanted to take things slow and leisurely to show her how much she meant to him. His hand wandered up to her full, luscious breast, and he gave it a little squeeze. As if his tongue had its own mind it flicked over the peak.

"Ummm," she let out a little whimper.

Their kisses went from urgent to savoring as their bodies tangled. Her breathing sounded as ragged as his own. The echo of his heartbeat resounded in his ears. His fingertips grazed the silky softness of her skin, up her thigh, and landed at the soft nestles of curls between her legs. Finding and tracing the sensitive area, he slipped a finger inside her wet center. She arched into his hand. He stroked her, steady at first and increasing pressure as he pleasured her. Languidly heating her up, making her melt like butter in the sun.

Lost in her soft mews, he added another finger taking her to the edge of orgasm and slowing his speed. When he ran his thumb against her clit, she arched up and moaned his name. He could feel her undulating against his fingers as he watched her come. Her face flushed. "You're gorgeous."

Palming him, she dragged her fingers along his length to the base. "And you're so hard." She pushed him onto his back and straddled him. "I need you inside me now," she said with a throaty whimper.

"Yes, ma'am."

Her eyes darkened with passion, and she dropped down on his cock. Nothing was better than joining with her. He thrust upward to make it even better. Needing to taste her, he pulled her head down to his and kissed her open and deep and hungry like a man who couldn't get enough of her. His hands enjoyed the feel of her breasts and her soft skin.

Heaven. She was his heaven. His nirvana. His everything.

He watched her closely while he buried himself inside her, stroking the warm wet walls that hugged him. Easing in and out in an unhurried rhythm which crescendoed into a frenzy of hard driving thrusts gaining speed and depth.

Her breathing grew more ragged, and he could tell she was close. He stroked gently while rocking deep inside her.

Arching her back, her body convulsed against him. She cried and bucked her hips. “Oh, Zack.” Her tremors quivered against him.

One more thrust and he set off like a rocket with a release that seemed to detonate with spasms as energy drained from his body. “Sunshine, that was ...”

“Mind blowing,” she said with a contented sigh.

“Out of this world.” Grinning like an idiot, he rolled her on his side and brought her body against him. “You own my heart.”

“Good to know.” She snuggled into the crook of his arm. Her breathing shallowed and she drifted off to sleep.

CHAPTER 43

An hour later, Zack held Birdie's hand as they walked into the back of the house. This incredible woman loved him and promised to marry him.

Ursula must've heard the door squeak open because she jumped up from her chair and rushed over to them. "I take it everything went well?"

Birdie's cheeks reddened to a pretty shade of pink. Then she held up her left hand with a shiny diamond. "We're engaged."

"That's frigging fabulous." Ursula launched herself at Birdie and threw her arms around her friend. "I'm so happy for you guys."

"Thanks," Birdie and Zack said at the same time.

"I can't wait. I've always wanted to be a bridesmaid."

Ursula clapped her hands several times. "Have you picked a date?"

"Today," he quickly said.

"We can't get married today," Birdie shrieked. "I mean, we need a license. It's Saturday, and I'm pretty sure the courthouse is closed on weekends."

"Can't we just stand up in front of a preacher?" Back in his day, the pastor would sign the church's registry.

"I don't think so." Birdie lifted a shoulder.

The last thing he wanted to do was push her into something she wasn't ready for. He put his arm around her shoulder. "Am I moving too fast? Your brother said you'll be on spring break in two weeks. We could head home and have the nuptials with your family?

"Hell, no. I'd much rather elope." Her impish smile said she was determined to do things her way. "The sooner the better."

His pulse hummed through his veins. He couldn't wait for her to be his bride. "Then we'll find a way."

"Too bad we're not closer to Vegas." Birdie's mouth tipped downward. "I'm pretty sure they have same day weddings. I wonder if there's a service like that near us."

Ursula grabbed her tablet and started tapping on the keyboard. "Give me a sec." She swiped her screen. "Heritage Wedding Chapel. Same day marriages."

"Where's that?" Birdie asked.

"On the border of Wyoming about forty-five miles

north." Ursula pulled up a photo online. "What do you think?"

"It's great, but—" Birdie motioned to her rounded body. "I'd like to look nice, and the only clothing that fits are tunics and leggings."

"You could be wearing a gunnysack and still be the most beautiful woman around." Especially with that radiant glow that made her skin rosy.

"Awww. Think I might keep you awhile." Birdie pressed a kiss to his cheek.

"That's good because I'm not going anywhere."

"Still, for my wedding I want a dress that makes me feel pretty."

Ursula rubbed her hands together. "I've got an idea. Why don't we go to Timely Treasures? I bet we can find a vintage dress with a full skirt, and if it needs any alterations, I can do those on my sewing machine."

"I love that shop. You're a genius."

"I do my best." She turned to Zack. "What are you gonna wear?"

He shrugged. "A button-down shirt and jeans I guess."

"For your wedding day? You can do better," Ursula tisked.

"Any ideas for me?" He wanted to look his best for his gal.

"You should rent a suit at the men's shop on Moose Valley Boulevard." Birdie rested her hands on top of her belly.

"Is that store on the main drag as I came into town?"

"That's the one." Ursula stood and snagged her purse from the counter. "Then we'll meet back here and drive out."

Thanks to Kristy, Zack had a plan.

CHAPTER 44

Birdie sung along to Blake Shelton's "Nobody But You" as she rode in Ursula's car. Her thoughts got all mushy. She really did love Zack.

"You gonna tell Granny about the wedding?" Ursula asked.

"I don't know. Think I should call her?"

"You better. She'll be ecstatic."

"Okay." She got out her phone and turned down the radio.

"Birdie?" Granny's voice rose in surprise. "I thought you'd call tomorrow. Is something wrong?"

"Not at all. You won't believe this." Birdie couldn't help but smile. "Zack and I are eloping."

"Oh, my goodness. This is a surprise." She lowered her voice and paused not saying a word.

"I know, right?" Birdie twined her finger around a lock of hair.

"What did your dad say?"

"I haven't spoke with him. You're the first one I called." To be honest, she wasn't ready to speak with Dad.

"He's always dreamed about walking his little girl down the aisle."

"Way to make me feel guilty, Granny." It was bad enough admitting she was pregnant, but now she'd break his heart by getting married without him.

"I'm only telling you the truth." Granny cleared her throat." Anyway, he'll be happy you're with Zack. He's always liked him as have I."

"Good to hear."

"When's the wedding?"

"Today. Ursula's taking me to find a dress."

"Hey, Mrs. Kellogg," Ursula called out.

"Tell her, hi." Granny paused for a second. "How can you get married today if you don't even have a dress? Maybe you should wait till next weekend. Better yet, you could come home in a couple weeks when you're on break."

"I don't want to wait. I love Zack and want to be with him." Plus, going home wasn't an option for her.

"All right, honey. It's already eleven. Do you think you'll make it to the chapel in time? I'm assuming you're driving to Vegas."

"We found a chapel in Wyoming. It'll take about an hour to get there."

"Looks like you've got everything figured out," Granny said. "Are you happy?"

"Oh, Granny. I am." Birdie went on to tell her about the rose petals that led to a pop-up tent and how Zack got on one knee.

"How romantic. I'm really happy for you two."

"Thanks. That means a lot to me." More than words could say.

"I wish I could see the ceremony," Granny said.

"What if we FaceTime?" She turned to Ursula. "Do you think you could prop up your phone so Granny can watch the ceremony?"

"Sure. She can be your unofficial second witness." Ursula turned into the parking lot.

"I'd love that," Granny's voice cracked and knowing her, happy tears filled her eyes.

"But now that we're at Timely Treasures, we have gowns to try on," Ursula took an empty spot not far from the store. "Hop to it."

"Ursula can be such a drill sergeant sometimes," Birdie said softly into the phone.

"I heard that." Her friend stuck out her tongue.

Birdie couldn't help laughing. "I'll text you when we're on our way."

"Call your dad. He deserves to know about this."

"I will." And she planned to do just that. If only she could get up the courage.

Ursula hustled with determined strides through the

center aisle of the store packed on both sides with racks of clothing. "The gowns are along the back wall on the left."

Given her ball of a baby, Birdie had to turn sideways in a couple of sections to get by.

"You're getting married today!" Ursula pushed through several gowns and pulled one out. Looked at it and put it back on the rack.

A part of her still worried that she wouldn't be a good wife. She held up an off-white mermaid gown with puffy sleeves. "What'ya think?"

"No." Ursula scrunched her eyes. She took it out of Birdie's hands, put it back on the rack and showed her a sleeveless A-line gown. "I like this one."

"Me, too." Birdie pulled out a sparkly white gown with an empress style waist and added it to the others.

Ursula held up two more gowns and Birdie nodded.

"Ready to try these on?" Ursula asked.

"More than ever." And if luck were on her side, she'd find the right one.

AN HOUR LATER, Birdie had her dress. A floor-length sleeveless one with lace and beading on the bodice, while Ursula had picked out a light blue knee length dress with a flared skirt.

"I'm starving. How does a burger sound?" her friend asked.

"Perfect." They drove to Buck's Burgers and saw a long line at the drive in, so Ursula pulled into a parking space. "I'm going inside."

"Then I might as well call my dad while you're gone."

"Good luck." Ursula strutted away.

Birdie's hand's shook as she pressed his name.

"Hey, shortstop. What's up?"

Her mouth got as dry as the Mojave Desert and she cleared her throat. *Just go for it,* she told herself. "I'm getting married. Today."

"Today? Really?" His voice came out a little pitchy.

"Yes, Dad. I'm marrying Zack. The baby's father."

"Why the rush? Right, you're pregnant." He let out a sad laugh. "It's a modern age. You don't have to get married if you don't want to." He had her best interest in mind.

"I always thought you'd walk me down the aisle, but I don't want to wait."

"Are you sure? Marriage is a big deal."

"I love him." Just thinking about him made her smile.

"I want you to be happy."

"I am."

"Good."

She could see him now giving a nod of approval. "You're the best." She wished she could hug him.

"Are you moving back?" His tone got serious.

"No Dad. Zack's moving here."

"Jacob. You need to get ready for the Smith's party." Goosebumps traveled up her arms as her mother's voice reminded her father of their dinner plans. She'd made the right decision to elope. "What are you going to say to her?"

"Go get married. I'll take care of your mom," he whispered. She could hear his bootsteps on the tile which meant he was going to his room.

"I love you."

"Back at you. Do me a favor and get video coverage with your package. That way I can watch my little girl say her vows."

"I will. I promise." She hung up. Her eyes welled with jubilant tears at having Dad's approval.

CHAPTER 45

Birdie couldn't stop grinning as she and Ursula walked along the polished hardwood floor leading to the chapel's entrance. The skirt of her floor-length gown swirled around her legs. With her hair up in a chignon and a short lacy veil attached, she felt beautiful. She still couldn't believe she found the perfect dress on such short notice. For the first time in her life, she liked dressing up. She started humming the tune "When Love Finds You."

"Vince Gil's the best. Love did find you," Ursula sighed.

"It has. Everything's working out for us." It was as if fate had a hand in this trip. When they arrived, Zack told her this church reminded him of the one in his hometown. The simple whitewashed building with a tall steeple above the tower offered a step back in history. The name itself, the

Heritage Wedding Chapel, suited them. Old and new melded into their future.

Her hands trembled holding the bouquet of wildflowers. “I’m excited. It’s hard to believe I’m getting married.”

“It’s meant to be.” Ursula hugged her tight. “I’m gonna call Granny on FaceTime.”

“Good idea.”

“Isn’t this dress perfect?” Ursula scanned Birdie’s outfit with her phone.

“Honey, you’re stunning,” Granny said. “It’s so you. Sleeveless and simple with a hint of elegance. And the short veil makes your eyes sparkle.”

“Don’t make me cry?” She didn’t want to redo her makeup.

“I’ll try not to. Is that beading on the bodice?”

“It is. And there’s just a little bit of lace along the hem.”

Ursula moved her camera down.

“You’re the prettiest bride ever.” Granny’s voice lowered. “Make sure and take lots of pictures.”

“We added photos and a video to our wedding package.” For an extra hundred fifty dollars she’d get a link for everything online. “Show her your dress, Ursula. It’s really cute with those three-inch heels.” She took the phone.

Ursula twirled and her short taffeta dress billowed.

“Love it.” Granny cleared her throat. “I’m delighted to have Zack as a grandson.”

“You’d better be.” In a few minutes, she’d be saying her vows with the man of her dreams. Glancing around the foyer, she could see Zack at the front of the chapel rocking back and forth on his heels. Her gorgeous groom only did that when he was anxious. "I talked to Dad. He's okay with everything." Her eyes got misty.

"I figured he would be."

"Give me a sec to set up the phone near the front, Granny. Then I'll walk Birdie down the aisle." Ursula rushed through the open door and came back in a blink. "Ready?" Her friend offered her arm.

"More than ever."

The wedding march played.

She stepped inside the chapel. Zack wore a black suit, white shirt, and bowtie. Love shone in his eyes as they locked on hers. The corners of his mouth lifted into a wide smile.

Hells bells if she didn't swoon a little. Luckily, she held onto her bestie or she might have stumbled because her legs were pretty wobbly.

"She's all yours." Kristy handed her to him.

An older man in wire-rimmed glasses clasped a bible. A gray-haired woman moved into a spot on the other side of Zack.

"Hello, sunshine." He winked at her. "You look mighty fetching."

"Back at you." Her heart beat a little faster.

"Fetching, huh?" He quirked a brow. "I'll take it."

The marriage officiant looked at Zack and Birdie. "Shall we start?"

He nodded.

"Dearly beloved. We are gathered here …"

All she could think about was this caring, wonderful guy who loved her. He really loved her.

The officiant cleared his throat.

Uh-oh. She was supposed to do something.

"Say I do," Zack whispered.

"To what?" She refused to say anything until she listened to the words.

"Do you, Roberta Kellogg, take this man to be your lawfully wedded husband, to love, honor, and cherish till death do you part?" The officiant eyed her as he repeated his words.

"Oh yeah, okay. I can do that."

The officiant gave her a sideways glance.

"I believe you're supposed to say, I do," Zack whispered.

"I do," her voice came out louder than she intended.

She heard Zack's husky snicker along with Ursula's giggle.

Granny let out a long guffaw and shouted, "That's my granddaughter."

"She's one in a million." Zack squeezed her hand.

Minutes later, she wore a gold band that matched the delicate diamond ring on her finger.

"You may kiss your bride," the officiant announced.

Zack leaned her backward and gave her a searing kiss. One filled with promises and love and everything that's right.

And just like that, Birdie became a married woman.

EPILOGUE

For the past year Birdie and Zack had been waiting for the right place, and this twenty-five-acre ranch practically fell into their lap thanks to a friend of her uncle's.

It came with a three-bedroom house that needed a little work. The kitchen appliances were avocado colored meaning they were ancient. But the master suite had its own bathroom complete with a clawfoot tub that she loved.

About an hour ago, they'd finished unpacking their last box and had already eaten dinner. Birdie gave her daughter her bath while Zack gathered the pizza and paper plates.

"I can't believe this is ours." After sharing a two-bedroom home with Ursula, they had their own space. Not that Birdie could complain. Ursula had been an excellent roommate.

"I know." Zack moved to an empty spot on the couch and kissed her on the cheek. He would continue working at the

Lazy 8 Dude Ranch while he built up his stock here. And she'd stay on at the school district. It'd take a lot of hard work to get this ranch up and running, but they had the rest of their lives to make it happen.

Violet sat on the floor with Duke at her side playing with the buttons on her interactive toy. When she pushed the one with a whistle sound, Duke barked and licked her face. "Doggie." She squealed with delight and wrapped her arms around his neck. Her brown eyes with flecks of gold had a mischievous glint reminding Birdie of Zack. She was already a charmer.

Violet let out a long yawn.

"Someone's getting sleepy," Zack said.

"It's been a busy day for all of us." Ever since they'd set up their new king-sized bed, her body tingled at the thought of trying it out with him.

"Bedtime." He scooped Violet in his arms.

"Dada." Her little girl smiled and sunk her head against his neck.

"She's definitely a daddy's girl." Birdie snatched the white stuffed cat who was missing an ear. "Better not forget Marshmallow." She handed the toy to her daughter.

"It's a good thing it didn't get lost with the move." Zack grabbed her favorite story, *Kurious Kats,* and eased into the chair still holding Violet. They rocked to a steady rhythm. Talk about frigging sweet. "Marshmallow and Taffy were good little cats," he read.

"Mar-mar." Violet pointed to the white cat who could be a ringer for her own cat.

Birdie looked around the room and admired her work. Last week with the help of Ursula, they turned this room into a child's paradise by painting it yellow and decorating the walls with duckies and kitties and puppies.

Zack continued rocking her as he read. It didn't take long for Violet to close her eyes. "She's plum tuckered out," he whispered, set her in her crib, and kissed her on her cheek.

"Which means she'll hopefully sleep soundly through the night." And they'd have lots of time to enjoy that new bed.

He feathered kisses along her neck. "Have I told you today how much I love you?"

"Several times."

"Good." His mouth captured hers. The taste of his hot and hungry tongue stroked and tangled with hers. She gave in to the delightful madness.

Meow. Hiss.

He pulled away. "What the heck?" Marshmallow ran past the couch and leaped into the windowsill. Duke rushed below the cat, wagging his tail. "Lie down." Zack motioned to the plush dog bed.

The dog slunk away.

"Poor Duke. He just wants to play." Zack tugged her closer.

"Give them time. At the other place, they seemed to have decided on a truce." Zack rubbed circles on her shoulders.

"True enough. What a family we have here."

"The best." Her gaze narrowed on his face. "Do you have any regrets about being in this time?"

"None. I've had the opportunity to live in the best of both worlds. Now I'm married to a modern woman who fulfills all my fantasies." Nipping her ear, he gave tender caresses from her neck to her cheek and stole a few more kisses from her obliging lips.

She brushed her fingertips along his forearm and swirled heat across his skin wherever she touched.

"You're sweeter than lemon drops."

"You and your sweet tooth." She scrunched her nose.

"Can't help it. I like tasting sweet things." He tasted her mouth, trailed love bites from the corner of her mouth to her jaw, and her breath hitched.

The openness of his gaze caused her lungs to seize for a second. She skimmed her nails into the muscles at his sides.

"If I ever meet up with the time travel gods, I'm gonna thank them for sending me to you. They changed my life for the better."

"Best decision in all of history." She covered his heart with her palm.

"Are you ready for bed?" his voice came out low and throaty.

"With you, always." She gazed greedily at him, memorizing every detail of his face. The rapid thrum of his pulse beat against her. Fire shot through her veins with the need to touch him everywhere.

"I plan to show you a good time."

"Yes, please."

He swept her up into his arms and carried her to their bed. Their life. Their happily ever after.

The End

TIME TO SAVE A COWBOY

If you enjoyed TIME FOR CHANGE, you might want to read TIME TO SAVE A COWBOY from my Western Romance Time Travel Series.

TIME TO SAVE A COWBOY shows that anything is possible when love is involved.

Captivated by the story of a cowboy hanged as a horse thief in 1890, an independent, modern-day woman travels back in time with only thirty days to save an innocent man.

Haunted by an old article about a man hanged over a hundred years ago, Mia Kellogg boards an old steam locomotive and plows right into the arms of the handsome cowboy Dusty Mann. Knowing time is of the essence, her problem is convincing her cowboy he's in danger?

Dusty Mann works as a foreman but is determined to buy his own ranch.

He doesn't need a modern, straightforward woman to barrel into his life or knock his plans off track.

But Mia steals his heart—and then claims she's from the future.

Read an excerpt from TIME TO SAVE A COWBOY

TIME TO SAVE A COWBOY EXCERPT

The server handed her a glass of water. She took a sip. “It’s warm.”

“No surprise. This is the desert.” The cowboy’s drawl didn’t seem practiced.

“I’m not as freaked as—” She looked at him, really looked at him, and recognized those wide-set gray eyes from somewhere. “You look familiar.”

“I’d remember meeting a pretty gal like you.” His smile lit up his handsome face, and her heart fluttered.

She focused on the people at the front desk. A clerk slid a key to a man, and he left with a lady in a long chiffon dress. Most likely people from the train.

A heavy-set woman approached her. “I’m Jenny Hayes. My husband, Bob, and I manage the hotel.”

“Mia Kellogg.” She held out her hand.

Jenny gave her a sideways glance.

Why wouldn't she shake her hand? Must be a germaphobe.

"Saw Dusty walk you in. Did the heat get to you?"

"Maybe a little. I'm fine now." Mia examined his features. His tan complexion set off his wolf gray eyes. He was a ringer to the cowboy from the picture in the antique shop. "Your name's Dusty?"

He straightened and rewarded her with a mischievous grin. "Yep."

"His given name's Harold Mann, but folks have been calling him Dusty since he was knee high to a grasshopper." Jenny butted in. She must be related to him somehow. "What brings you to our town?"

"A short vacation."

"Well, you certainly chose an ideal time for your stay. Tomorrow's our monthly ball." Jenny's cheeks reddened.

Now Mia was confused. She and Birdie had tickets for the Daggett dance. Maybe she got the name of the town wrong. Still, if her relatives were here, she should have seen them by now. "Could I borrow your phone and call my cousin?" Mia asked, anxious to talk with someone she knew.

"Golly, we don't have a telephone here. Our general store is the only business in town that has one. The shop's closed 'till morning," Jenny said.

Mia's throat got tight. Only one phone in town. This took the turn-of-the-last-century thing a bit far.

"I imagine you're famished, miss. May I find you a table in the dining room?"

"Please." Starved, at least her stomach didn't rumble.

Jenny turned to Dusty. "Will you be joining Miss Kellogg?"

Mia expected him to refuse politely. Not say, "I'd be honored." He stood and offered his arm. His scent of leather and masculinity made her lean closer. Wrong response for a guy she'd just met.

Jenny led the two of them through the spacious ballroom. Mia's right foot hit a slick, polished spot on the hardwood flooring. "Oh no."

Dusty tightened his grasp on her arm. "Careful, darlin'."

Was her lightheadedness from lack of food or … was it him? She took small mindful steps to their linen-covered table. Mindful of the waxed floor. Mindful of clutching his muscular biceps.

"Here you go." He pulled out her chair. His gray eyes darkened when he looked at her. He appeared well-mannered, but she wondered if his kisses would hold a bad boy edge. She couldn't believe she thought about kissing him. Not exactly appropriate for a guy she barely knew—but he was cute.

Her eyes drifted to the five o'clock shadow on his chin. Certain she'd been caught staring, she unfolded her napkin and placed it on her lap.

"Enjoy your meal," Jenny said and scurried off.

Mia should be looking for her phone, but hunger won

out. She knifed jelly on a roll and bit into the warm orange-flavored dough. Wickedly scrumptious. She drank from a crystal glass. "The lemonade's sour." A pound of sugar wouldn't take away the tartness.

He held up a crystal bowl. "Want some sugar?"

"Please." She should use Sweet'N Low but being on vacation why not splurge a little? She added three generous teaspoons, deciding she'd make up for her indulgences at spin class on Monday. "What do you do?"

"Do?" His brow rose, and he looked at her like she asked him to explain the theory of relativity.

"Your job."

"Me? I'm a cowhand." His drawl came out a bit over-exaggerated.

Her dad regularly watched old westerns. This guy had a casual Gary Cooper presence. She focused on the jagged scar on his chin. She liked the flaw, showed he wasn't plastic-perfect. "Where's your ranch?"

"It's not mine." He winced for a flash. "I'm the foreman of Los Flores Ranch."

The hot cowboy sitting across from her lived in the next town over. Moving back to her hometown suddenly had a big advantage, namely him. She could see him working on the ranch on the outskirts of Hesperia. Lifting bales of hay would explain his beefy arms.

She'd have to give him her number before she left.

TIME TO SAVE A COWBOY

COWBOY'S CUPID

If you enjoyed TIME FOR CHANGE, you might want to read COWBOY'S CUPID from my Love's Magic Series.

A Forbidden Love

When Cupid's arrow accidentally strikes the wrong cowboy, she's supposed to fix her mistake—not fall for the alluring mortal.

Cami Calypso receives her first assignment just in time for the Valentine season. As a newbie Cupid Archer, her life is perfect until her arrow accidentally strikes the wrong man. She has sixty days to secure a job as his housekeeper on a ranch and find the cowboy his soul mate—not keep him for herself.

Rhett Holloway needs a housekeeper and cook.

He doesn't need an adorable blonde to distract him.
He doesn't need her to fix his love life.
But here she is, and he finds her irresistible.

Read an excerpt from COWBOY'S CUPID

.

COWBOY'S CUPID EXCERPT

Rhett had a strange feeling in his gut during dinner. Cami kept checking her watch. He'd asked what bothered her, but she said everything was fine.

After a long day, he helped her clean up the dinner dishes, and they walked to her apartment. Her stance was rigid, her body tense. She didn't shift toward him as he strode with his arm around her shoulder.

"What's wrong?"

"I need to tell you something." She shrugged but wouldn't look at him.

They'd only known each other close to two months, but his heart was all in. He unlocked the apartment door. Seated at the edge of the couch, Cami put a distance between them and avoided eye contact.

"Go ahead." He stood by the kitchen table and waited for a response.

"We were never meant to be together," she said, still not looking his way.

His chest tightened. She was breaking up with him.

"I've got a secret. When I show you, I hope you'll still love me."

"Whatever you've done in the past doesn't matter. We'll get through it." He'd made his share of mistakes.

She extracted a glass vial from her pocket. It sparkled and shimmered. "It's not what I've done, it's what I am."

"What are you?" He didn't even see a flicker of a smile.

Her lips tightened into a grimace. "Please listen carefully to what I say."

"All right. Spill." He tapped the side of his pants.

She licked her lips and took a deep breath. "I told you I was a Cupid when you took me to the archery range."

"Okay."

She folded her arms. "I live in Zeus' Kingdom up in the clouds."

His teeth ground, as he sat next to her and said sarcastically, "Of course you do."

"You've seen my archery skills. Even said I was talented." She lifted her chin and blew out a breath. "I am a Cupid, a real live Cupid."

"That's crazy." Maybe she was crazy. His primal instinct told him to leave, but he couldn't move.

"My occupation is an archer." Tears pooled in her eyes. "I'm telling you the truth."

"If you're leaving me, say so, and quit making up this lame story."

"I don't want to go anywhere." She twirled a curl around her finger.

"You don't? And here I thought you were breaking up with me."

"If only things were different. I've got to return home." She looked at her watch.

"So, you are leaving me? Why?" He was confused.

"I don't want to. I'm happy here." Her body slumped, her chin dropped. "My whole life I've dreamed of being good enough."

"But you are good enough." She was the best thing to ever happen to him. "You're perfect for me."

"Don't make me cry, please let me finish." Her eyes softened. "I've dreamed of visiting Earth and infusing humans with arrows of love. When I got my first earthly assignment, I hit the wrong man, namely you."

Those blue eyes. "You shot me with your arrow of love?"

"It was a mistake. My assignment ducked, and I hit you instead. I was sent to rectify my mishap and set you up with your soulmate. We were never supposed to fall in love."

"You love me." His spirits soared.

"Yes."

"'Bout time you admitted it." He moved closer, but she backed up, out of his reach.

"Will you accept the real me?"

"What do you mean? The real Cami's right in front of me."

"Watch." Rocking back and forth on her heels, her cheeks flushed to a rosier red.

His eyes riveted to her hands.

She unscrewed the glass vial and poured out a glittery substance. Iridescent pink dust swirled and surrounded her. Her body shrunk to the size of a doll, dressed in a shimmering gown. Iridescent wings formed at her shoulders. She flew up midway between the floor and the ceiling.

"Holy shit!" He stared, not frightened, confused.

"I'm a C-Cupid." Her words came out broken.

He froze, became immobile. "This can't be happening."

"I love you, always will." She hovered close to him, and he felt her lips kiss his cheek.

"It's unreal."

"Tell me about it." Her eyes were wide. Wary.

"You really are a Cupid?"

"Yes. Do you still love me?"

He didn't know what to think. "It's too much." He turned his back to her, put his head in his hands.

His girlfriend—a ruler-sized pixie. It couldn't be true.

Except he'd seen her.

COWBOY'S CUPID

BOOKS BY NIKI MITCHELL

Romance Novels by Niki Mitchell

Western Time Travel Series

TIME TO SAVE THE COWBOY

TIME FOR LOVE

TIMR FOR CHANGE

Love's Magic Series

COWBOY'S CUPID

REBEL'S CUPID

FIREBRAND'S CUPID

Standalone Books

LOVE'S HIGH TIDE

Audio Books

TIME TO SAVE THE COWBOY

TIME FOR LOVE

Children's Books by Niki Mitchell

KURIOUS KATZ

KURIOUS KATZ AND THE BIG MOVE

KURIOUS KATZ AND THE PLAY DAY

KURIOUS KATZ AND THE NEW FRIEND

KURIOUS KATZ AND THE BIRTHDAY PARTY

KURIOUS KATZ AND THE HALLOWEEN COSTUMES

KURIOUS KATZ AND THE CHRISTMAS TREE

KURIOUS KATZ AND THE BEST CHRISTMAS EVER

FOSTER CATS: ARTEMIS AND HER SNEAKY BROTHER HERCULUES

KURIOUS KATZ AND THE FOURTH OF JULY

KURIOUS KATZ AND THE VALENTINE SURPRISE

KURIOUS KATZ AND THE SNICKERDOODLE STORY

PRECIOUS PUPS: BREEZY GETS ADOPTED

DEAR READERS

Thank you for reading TIME FOR CHANGE.

I hope you enjoyed my story as much as I enjoyed writing it. Won't you please consider leaving a review? Even just a few works would help others decide if the book is right for them.

Best regards and thank you in advance.

Niki J. Mitchell

I look forward to hearing from my readers.

Visit me at https://nikimitchell.weebly.com/
Follow me on Facebook at author Niki J. Mitchell
Twitter Niki Mitchell@NikiMitchell7
Instagram NikiJMitchellAuthor

ABOUT THE AUTHOR

Niki Mitchell writes children's books along with contemporary fantasy and historical time-travel romance. She was born in Chicago, Illinois, and moved to Whittier, California in first grade. With a houseful of books and a local library located a few short blocks, her love of reading began at a young age.

Married for over thirty years and a romantic at heart, she enjoys writing about strong female characters in unusual settings. When she isn't playing with her cats, she enjoys reading, taking walks, water aerobics, photography, and traveling.

COPYRIGHT

Printed in the United States of America

www.ingramcontent.com/pod-product-compliance
Lightning Source LLC
Chambersburg PA
CBHW030356310726
48979CB00001B/323
* 9 7 8 1 9 5 1 5 8 1 2 6 8 *